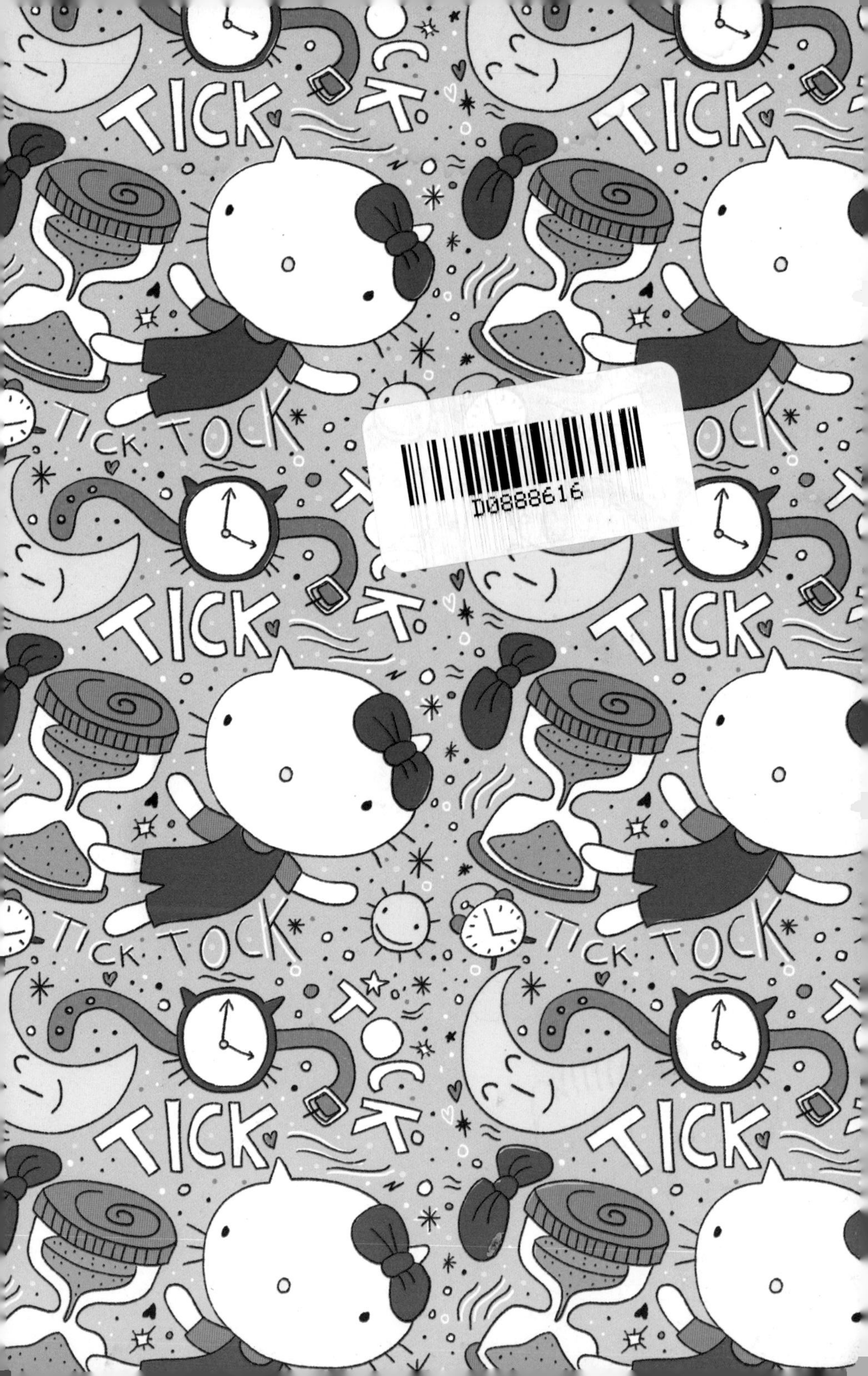
TICK
TICK TOCK
TICK
TICK TOCK
TICK

HELLO KITTY®
It's About Time

WITHDRAWN

stories and art by
Giovanni Castro, Jacob Chabot,
Ian McGinty and Jorge Monlongo

hello kitty shorts by
Erica Salcedo

HELLO KITTY®
It's About Time

Cover Art Jacob Chabot
Cover and Book Design Shawn Carrico
Editor Traci N. Todd

Printed in China

Published by VIZ Media, LLC
P.O. Box 77010
San Francisco, CA 94107

10 9 8 7 6 5 4 3 2 1
First printing, February 2015

"Beach Party," "Ahead of the Game," "Dance Off" and "Sweet Treats"
Stories and art by Ian McGinty, colors by Fred C. Stresing

"The Race," "Cuckoo Clock" and "Birthday Surprise"
Stories and art by Giovanni Castro

"Mix Tape"
Story and art by Jorge Monlongo

"House Music," "Wednesday" and "All Day Long"
Stories and art by Erica Salcedo

Contents

Family and Friends 6

Beach Party 9

The Race 14

Ahead of the Game 19

House Music 24

Dance Off............................ 25

Mix Tape.............................. 30

Wednesday..........................40

Sweet Treats........................41

Cuckoo Clock 46

All Day Long 56

Birthday Surprise..................57

Creators 62

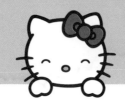

Family

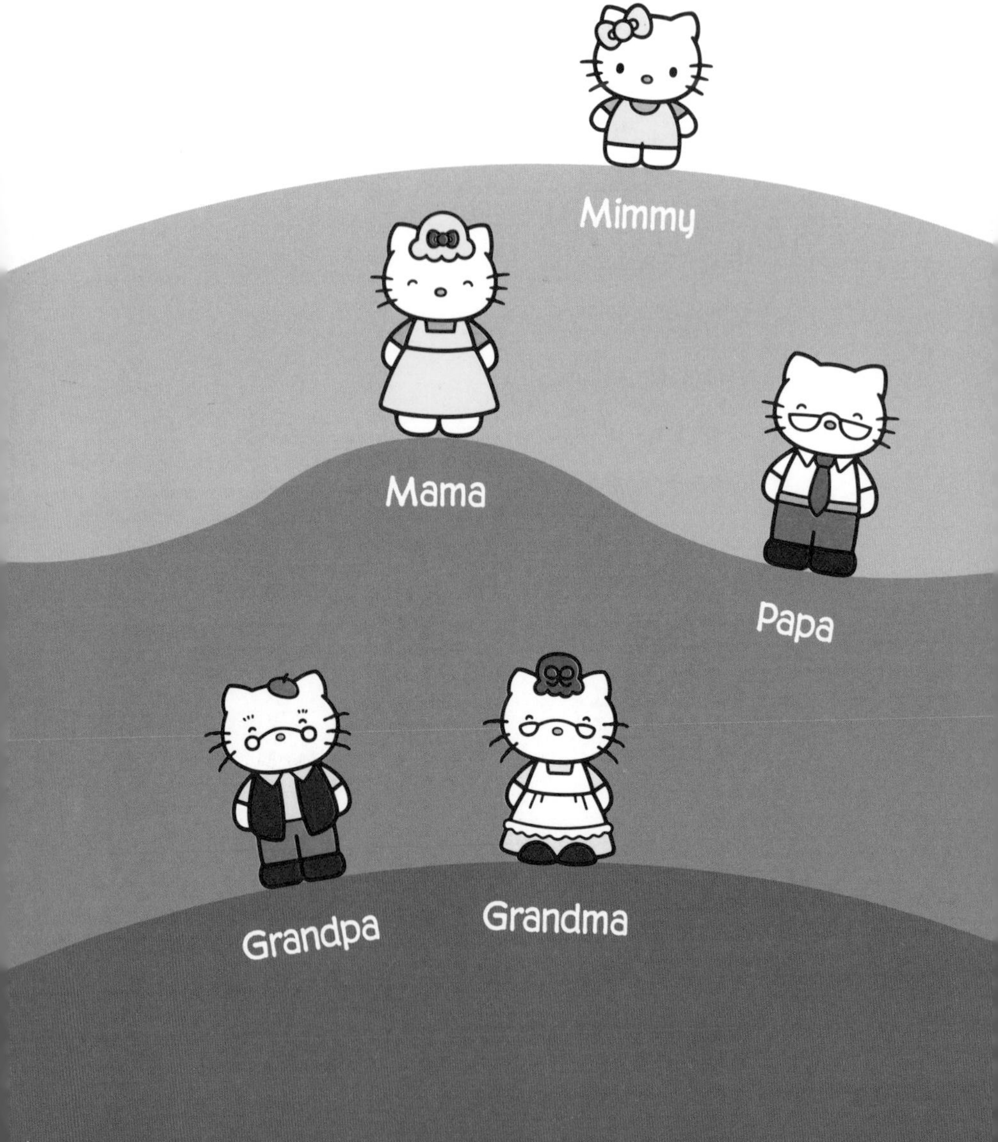
Mimmy
Mama
Papa
Grandpa
Grandma

and Friends

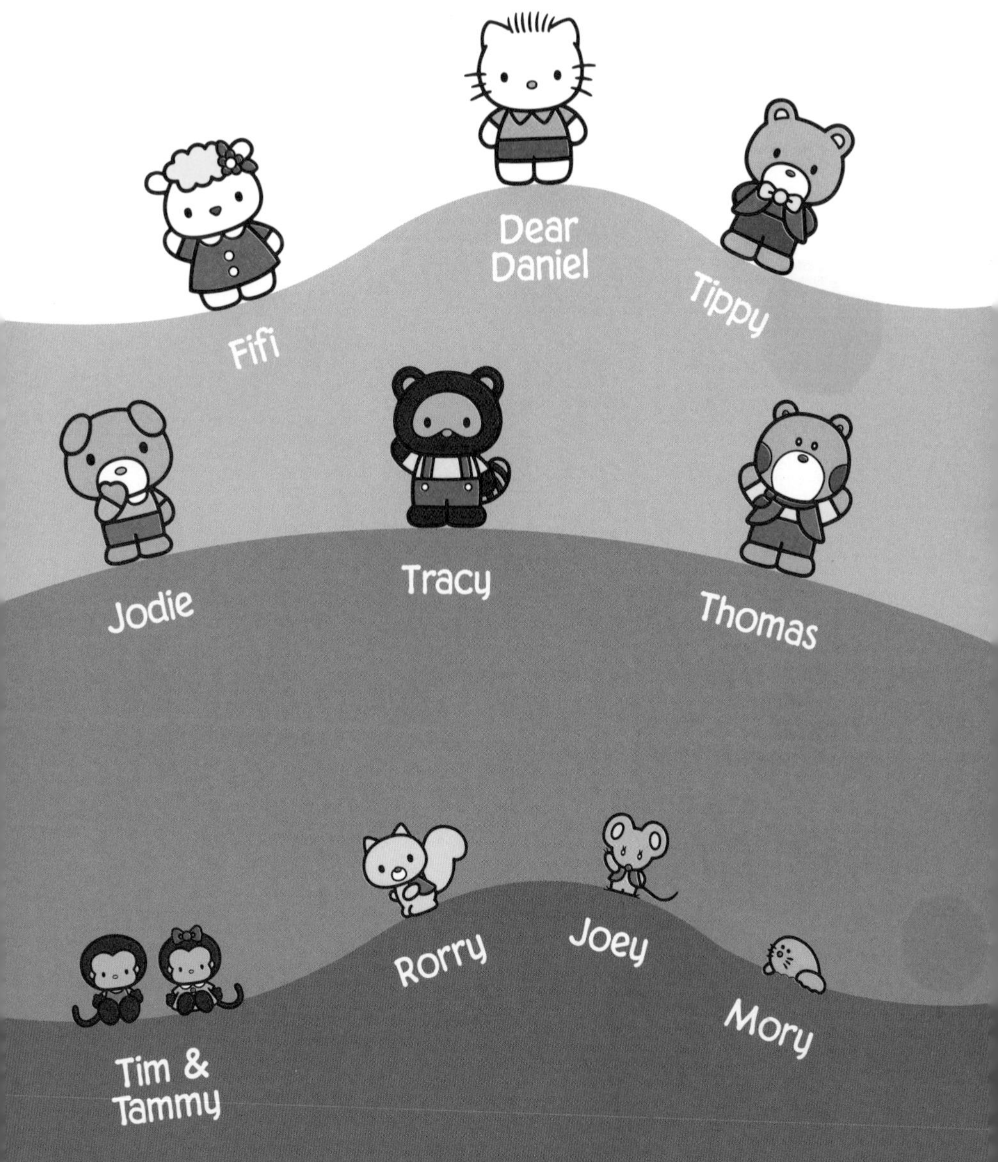

Dear Daniel
Fifi
Tippy
Jodie
Tracy
Thomas
Rorry
Joey
Mory
Tim & Tammy

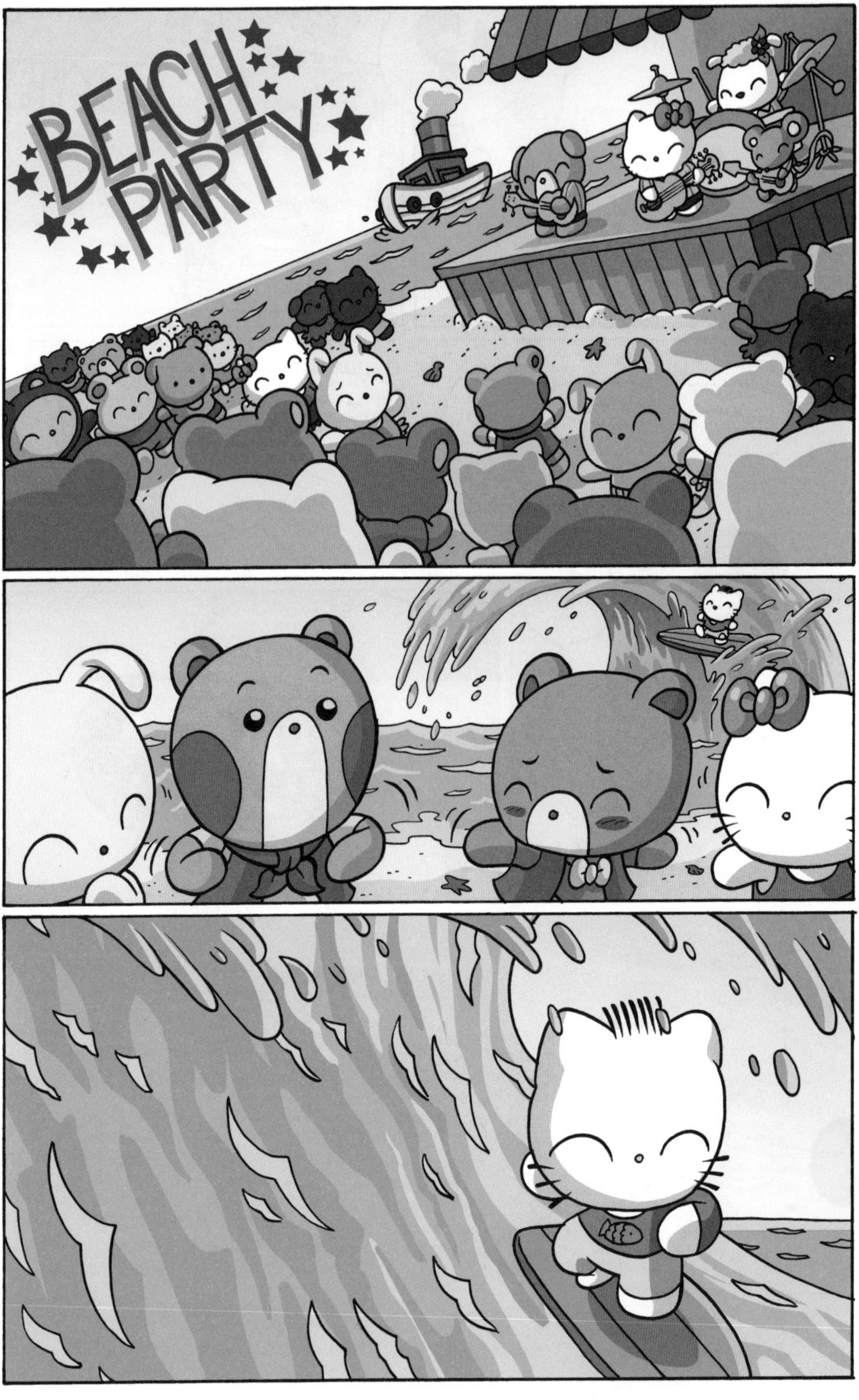
BEACH PARTY

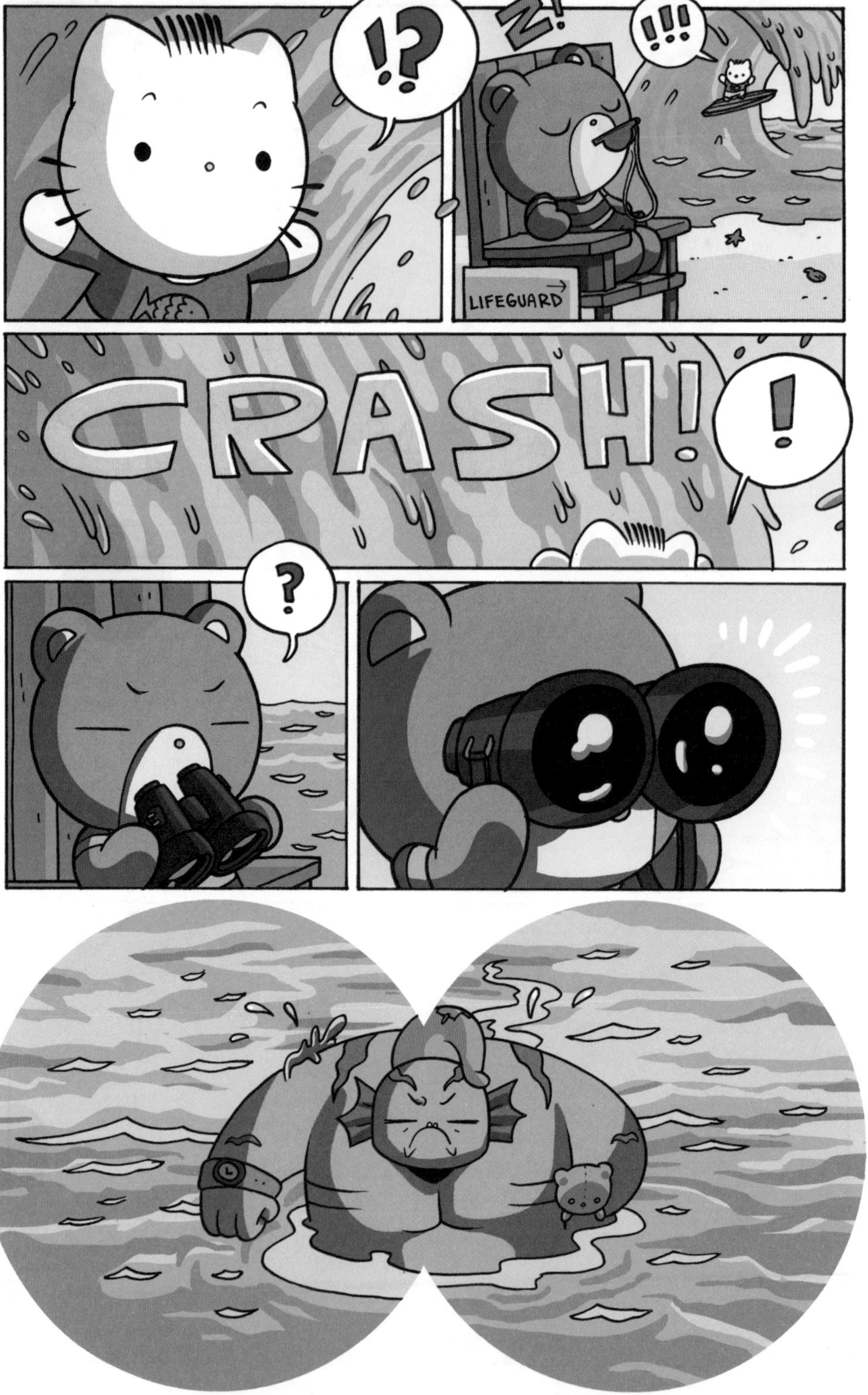
!?
Z!
!!!
LIFEGUARD
CRASH!
!
?

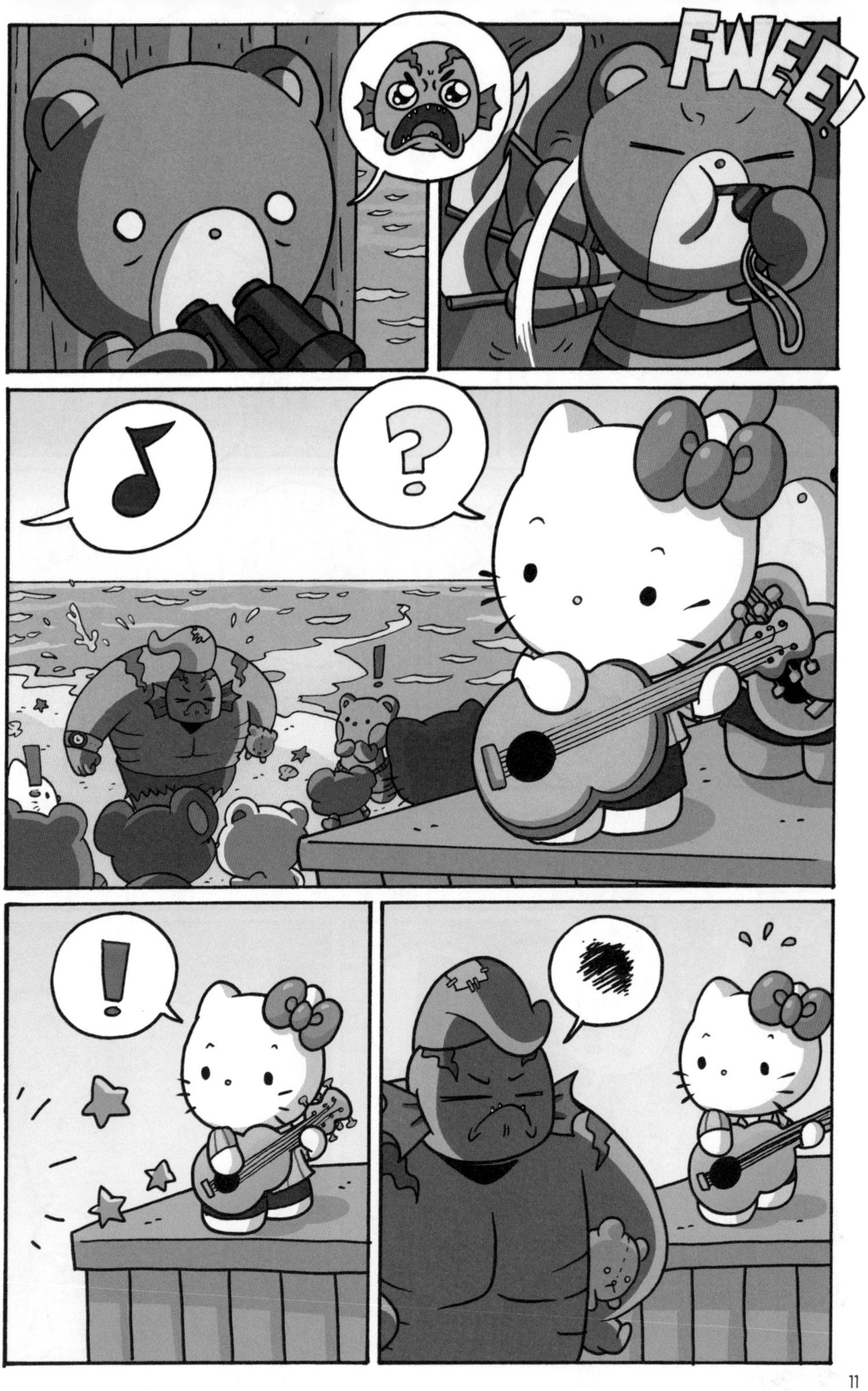
FWEE!
♪
?
!
!
!

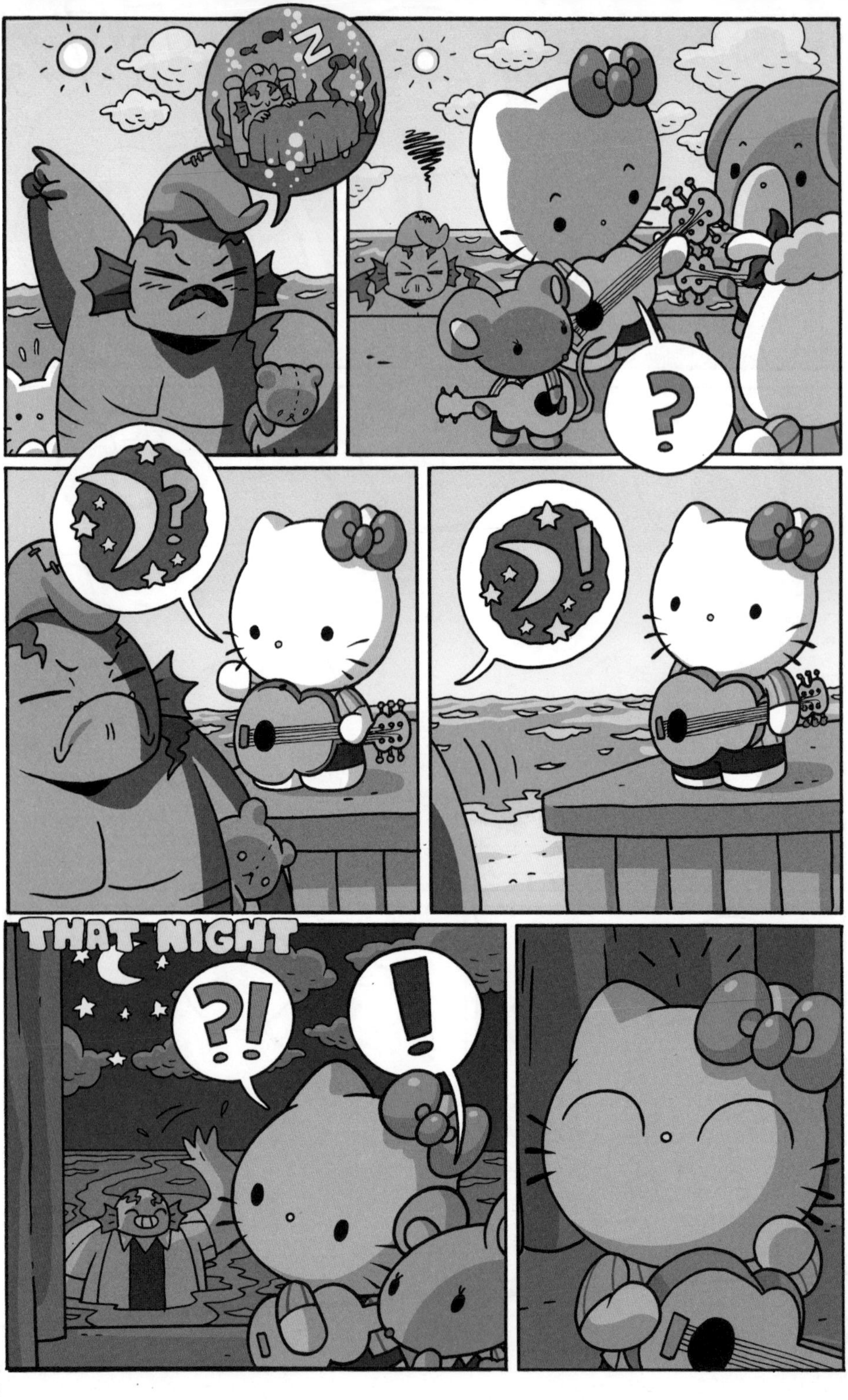
Z
?
?
!
THAT NIGHT
?!
!

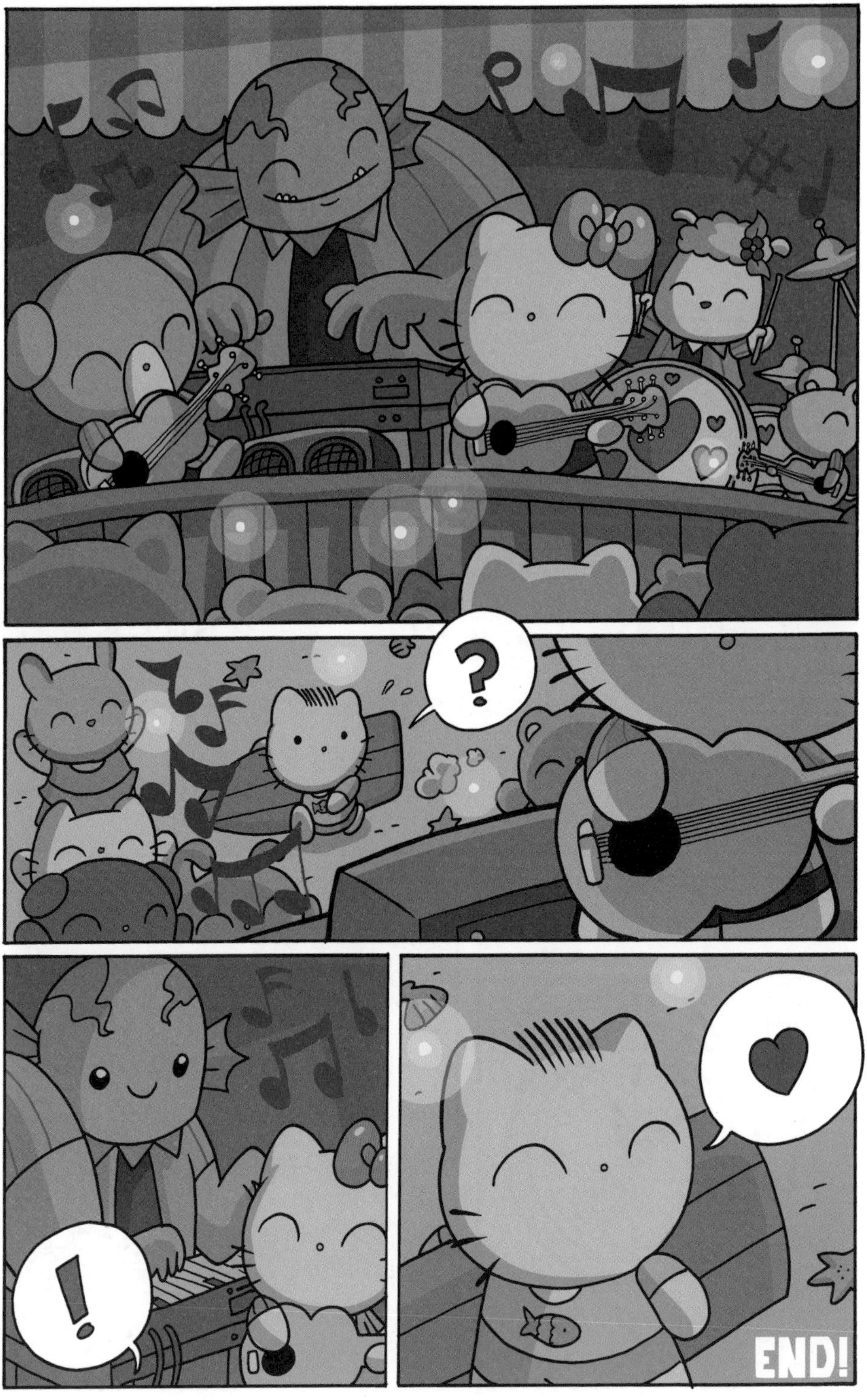
?
!
END!

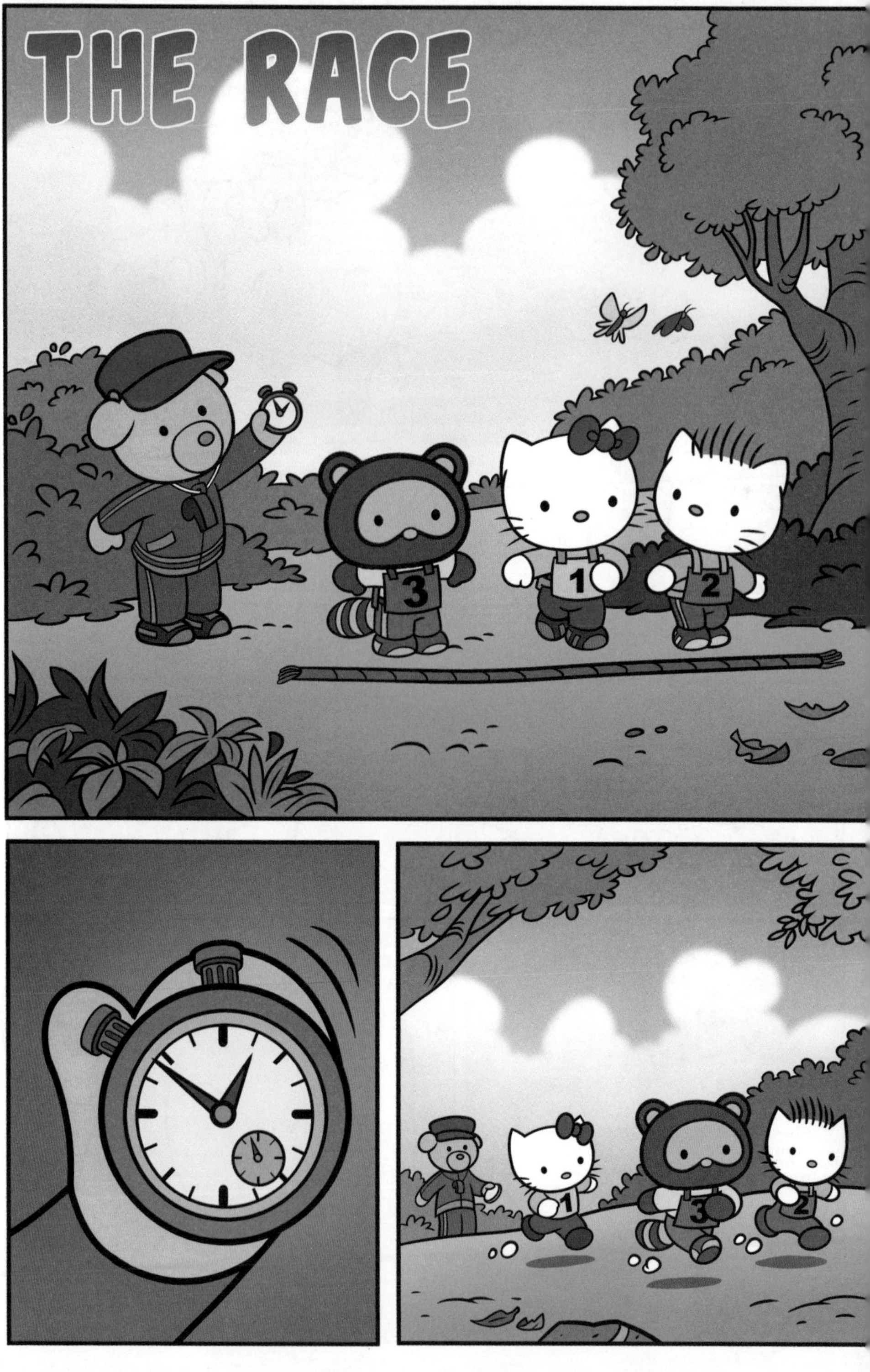
THE RACE

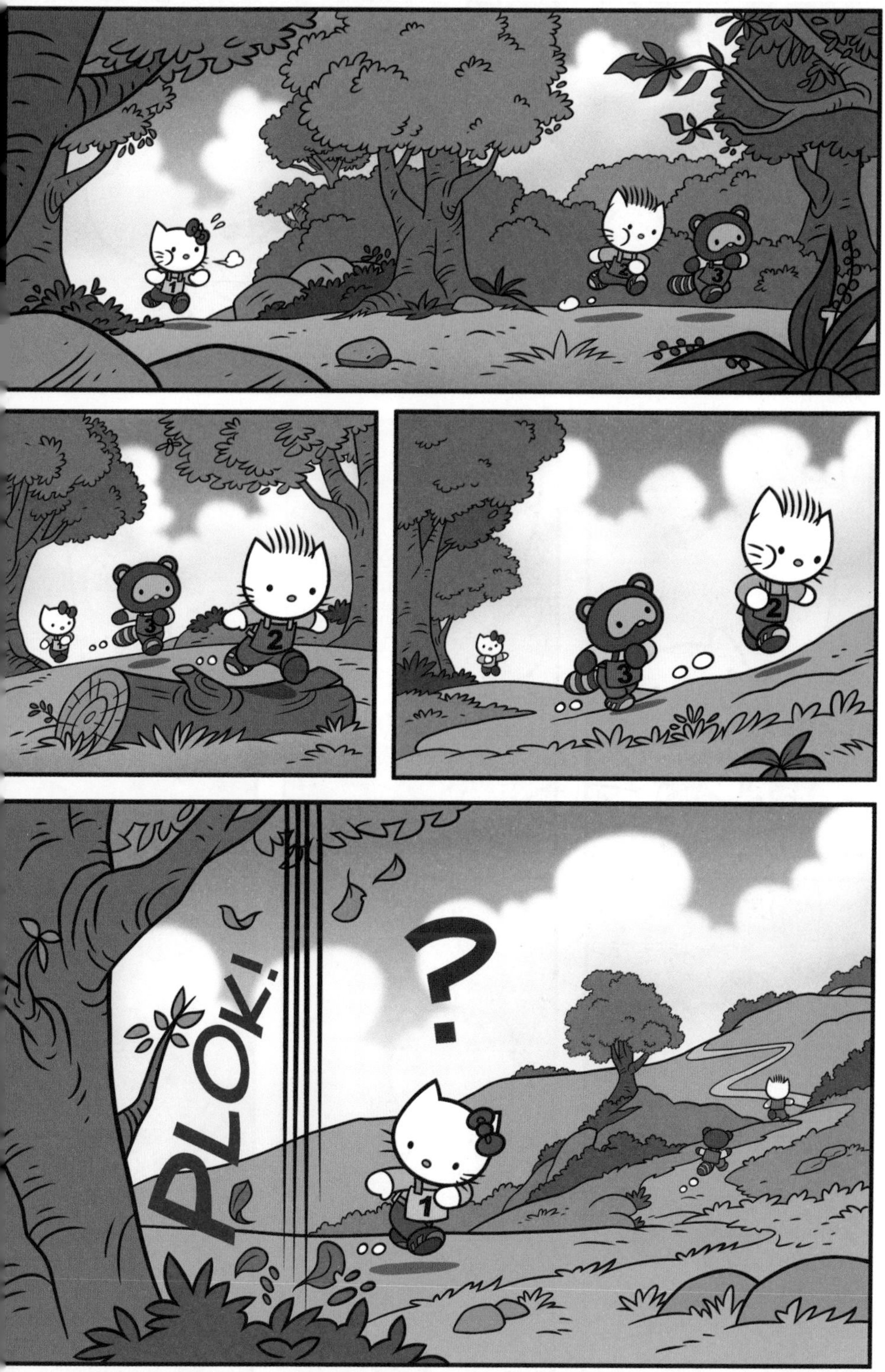
PLOK!
?

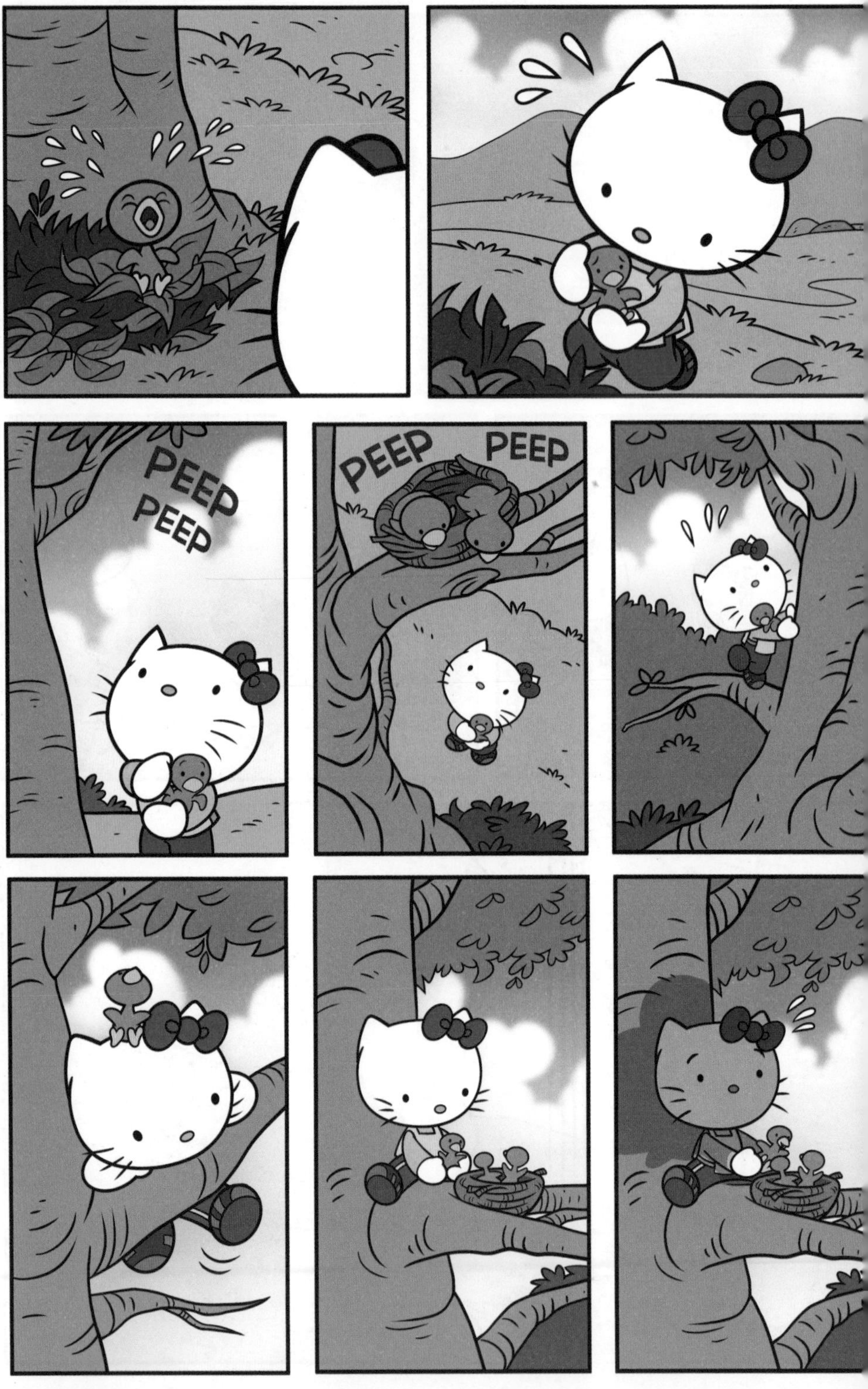
PEEP
PEEP
PEEP
PEEP

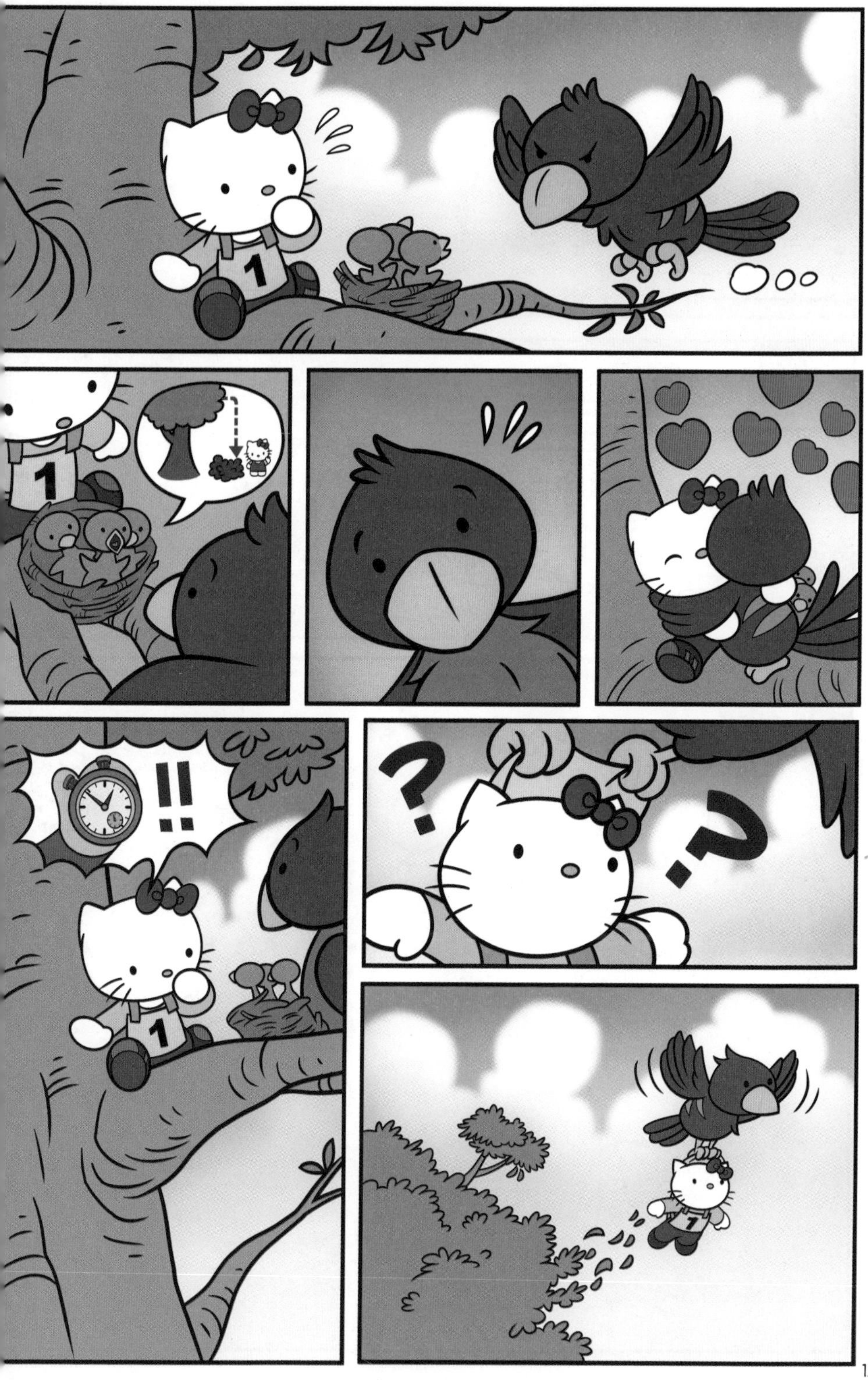
!!
?
?

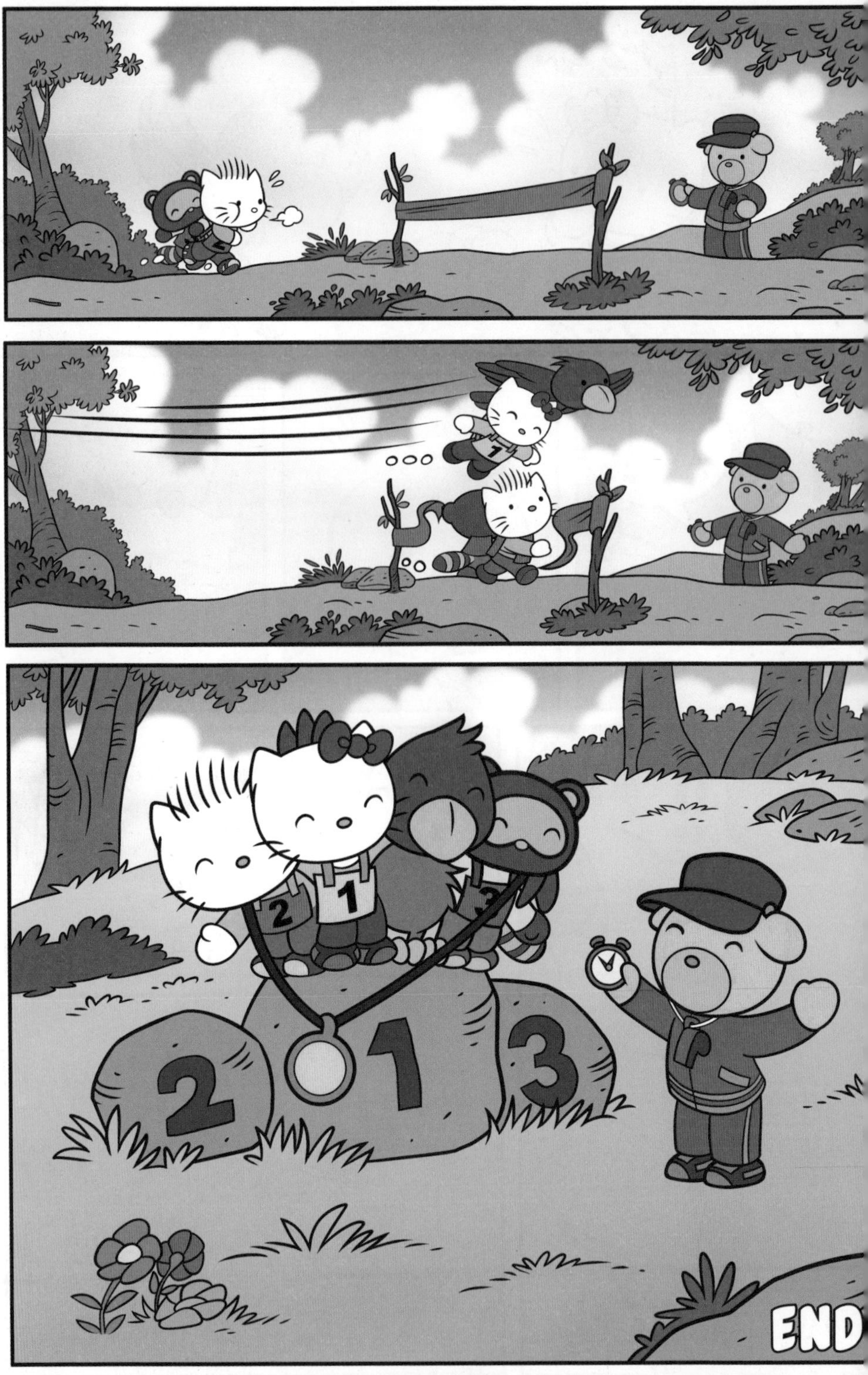
2
1
3
END

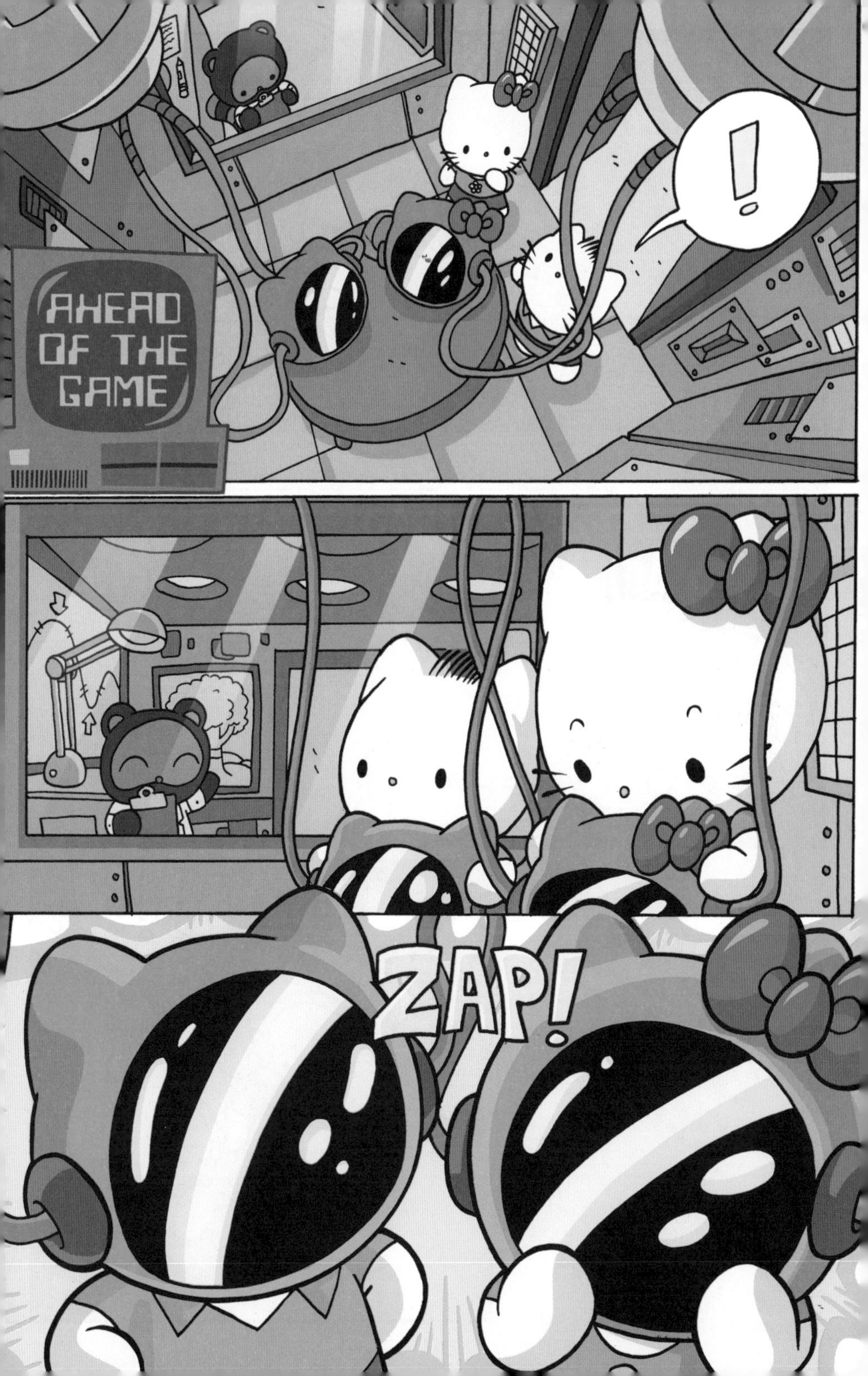

AHEAD OF THE GAME
!
ZAP!

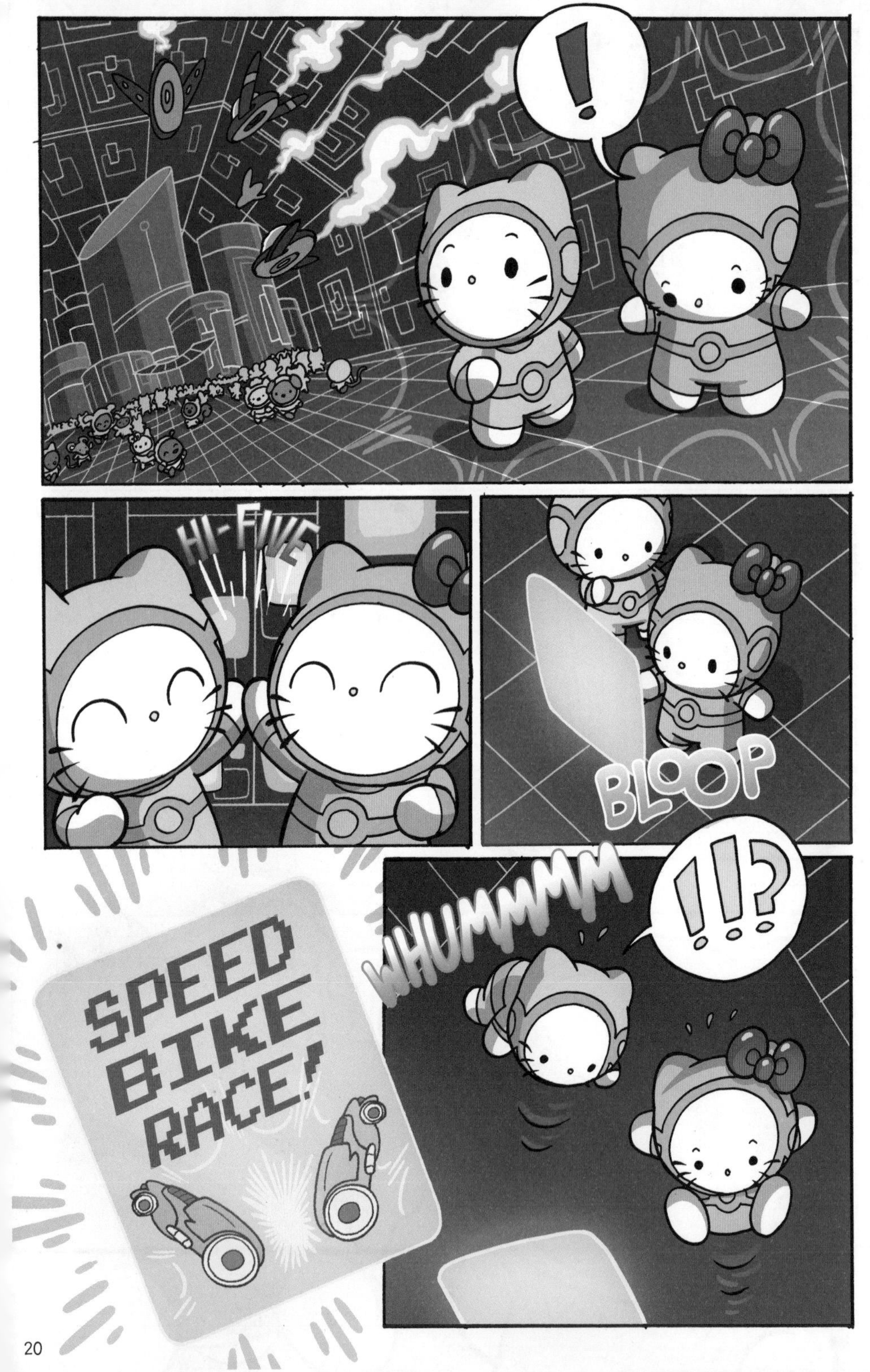
!
HI-FIVE
BLOOP
SPEED BIKE RACE!
WHUMMMM
!!?

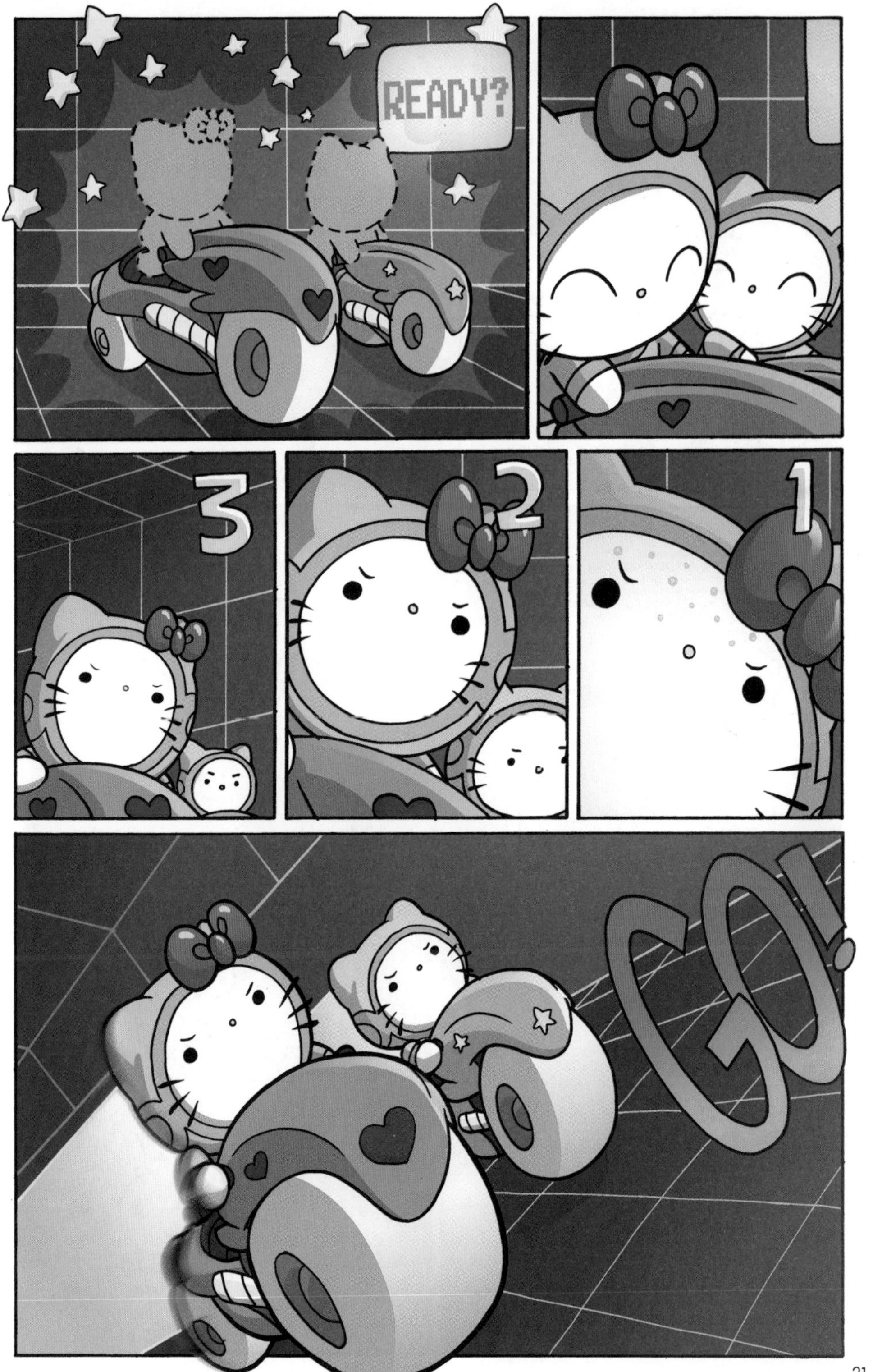
READY?
3
2
1
GO!

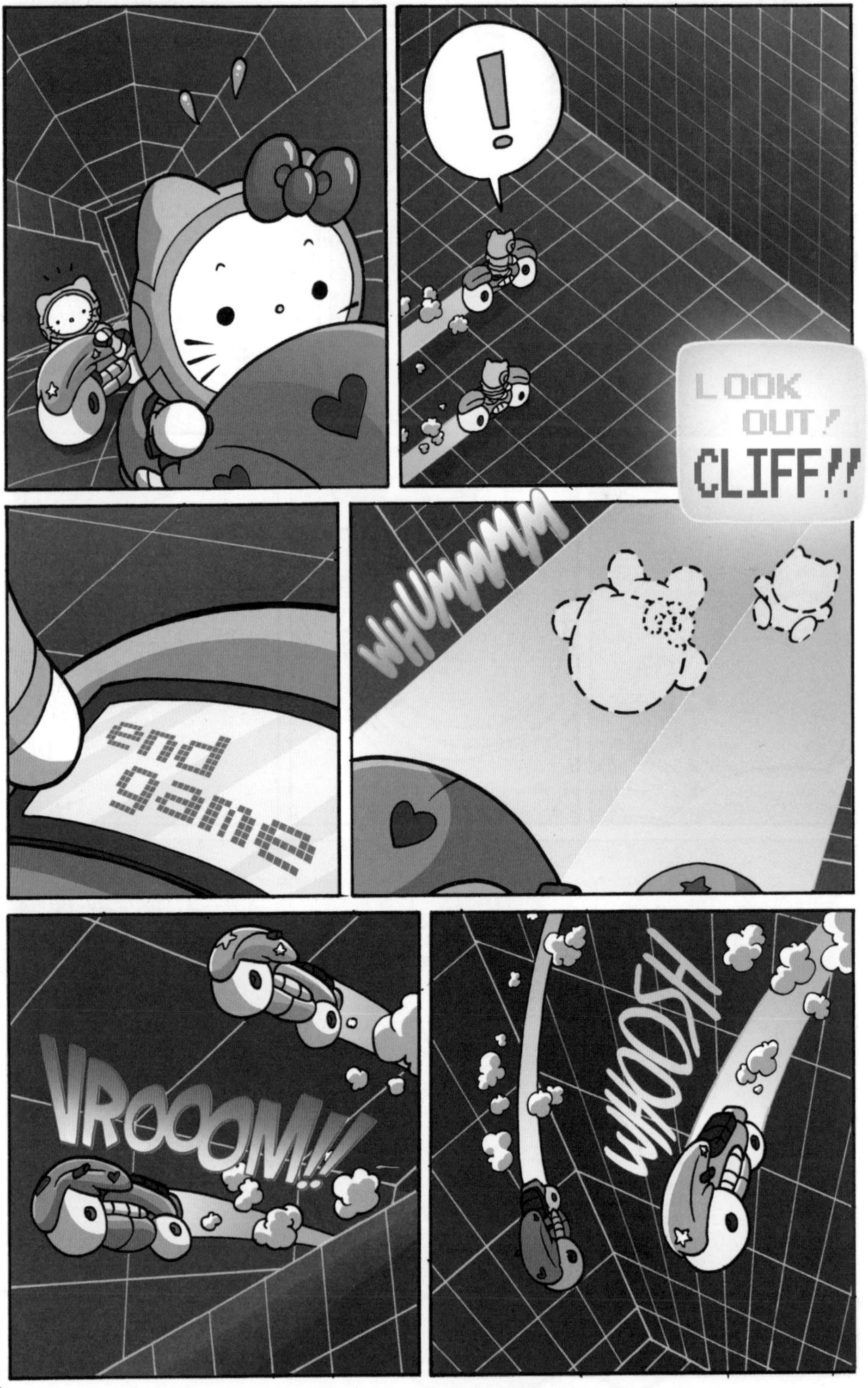
!
LOOK OUT!
CLIFF!!
end game
WHUMMMM
VROOOM!!
WHOOSH

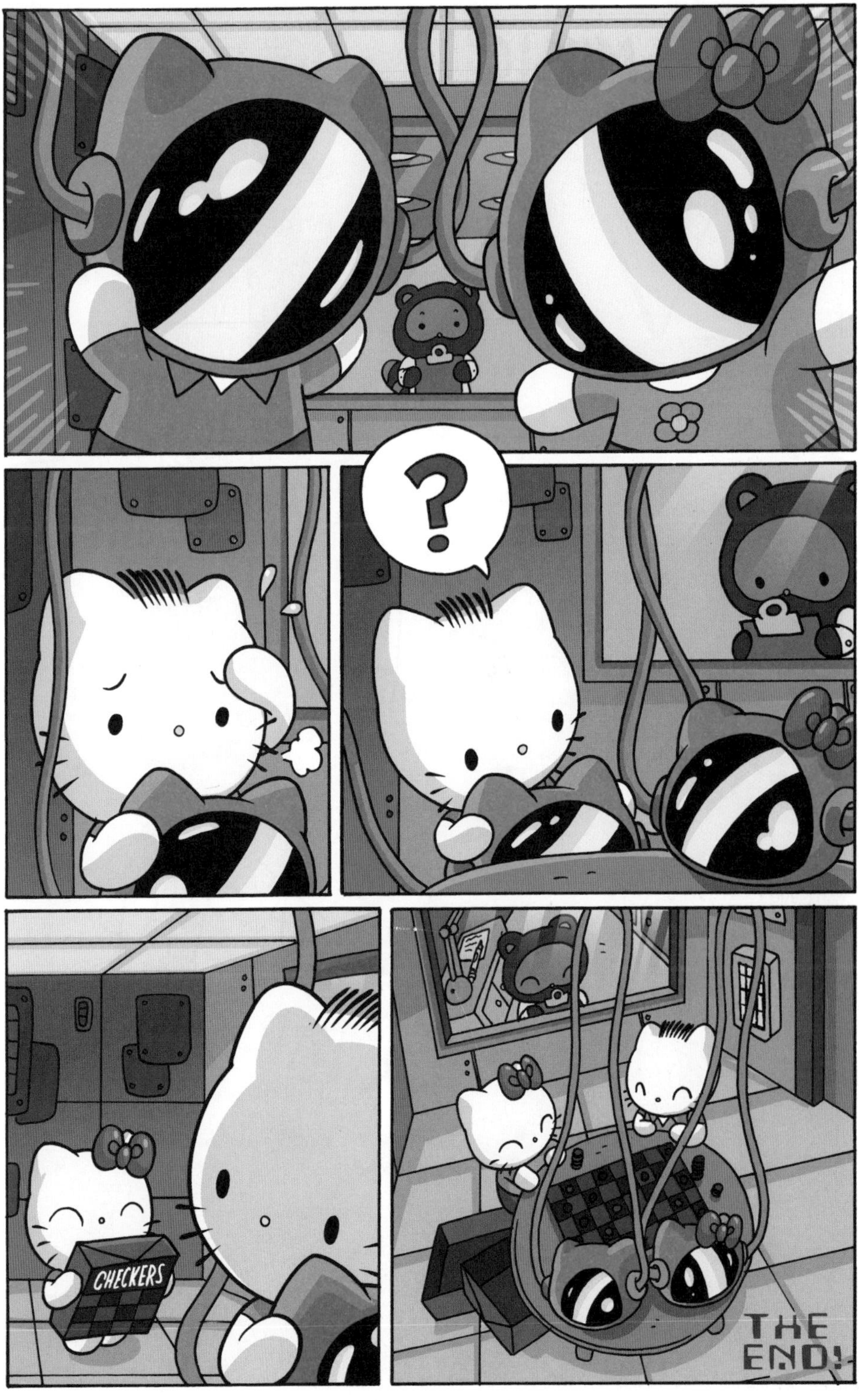
?
CHECKERS
THE END!

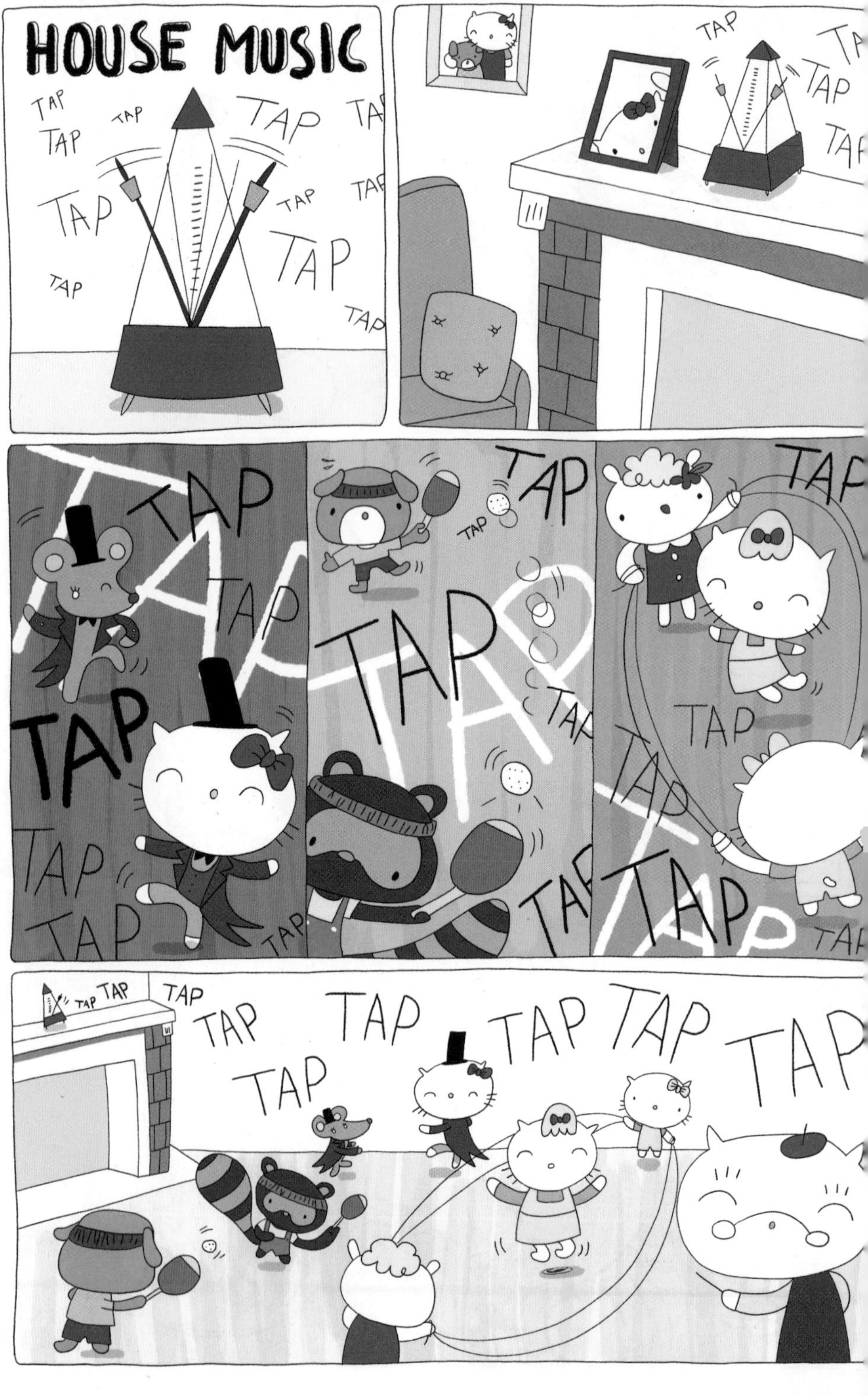
HOUSE MUSIC
TAP
TAP
TAP
TAP
TAP
TAP
TAP
TAP
TAP

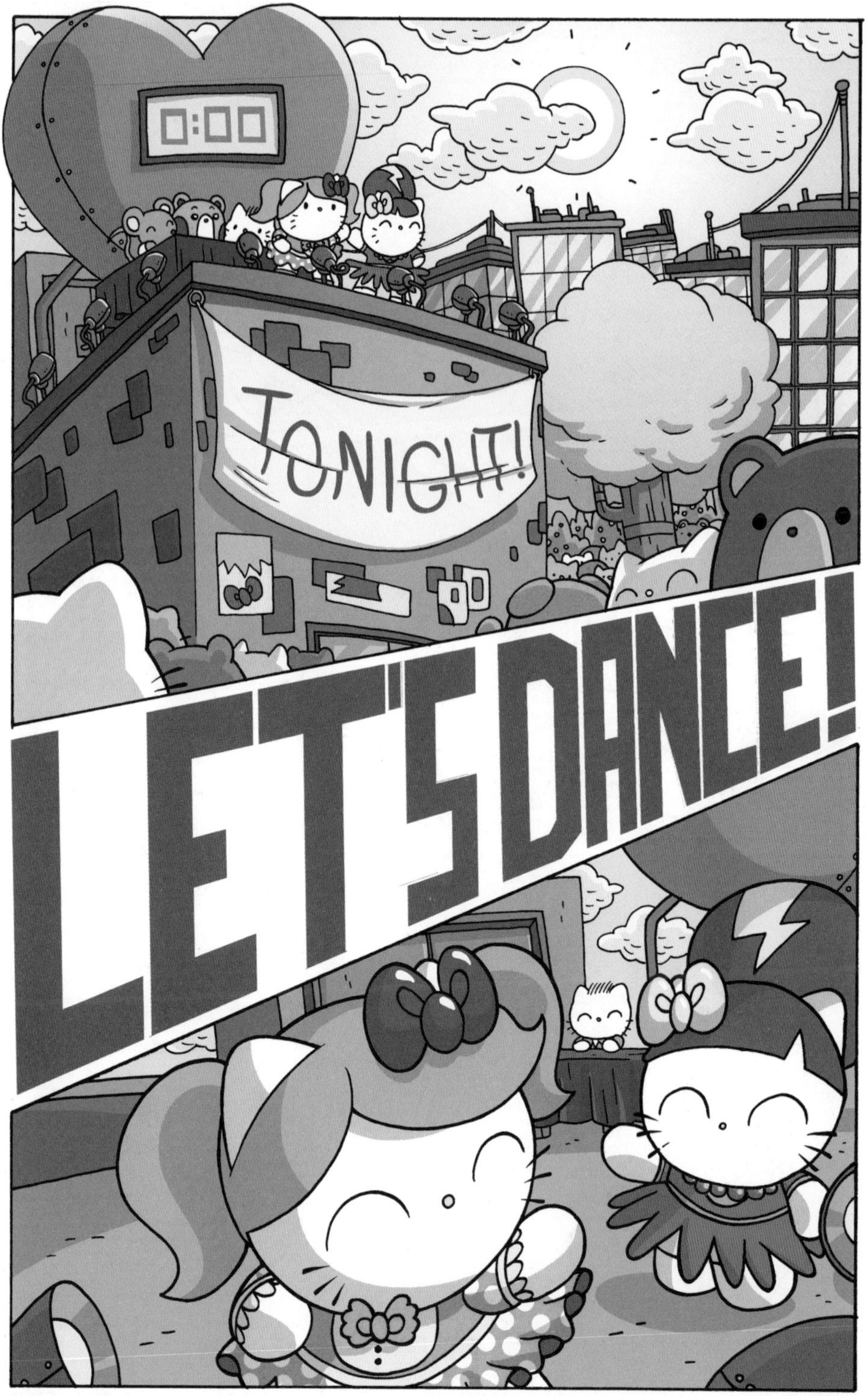
0:00
TONIGHT!
LET'S DANCE!

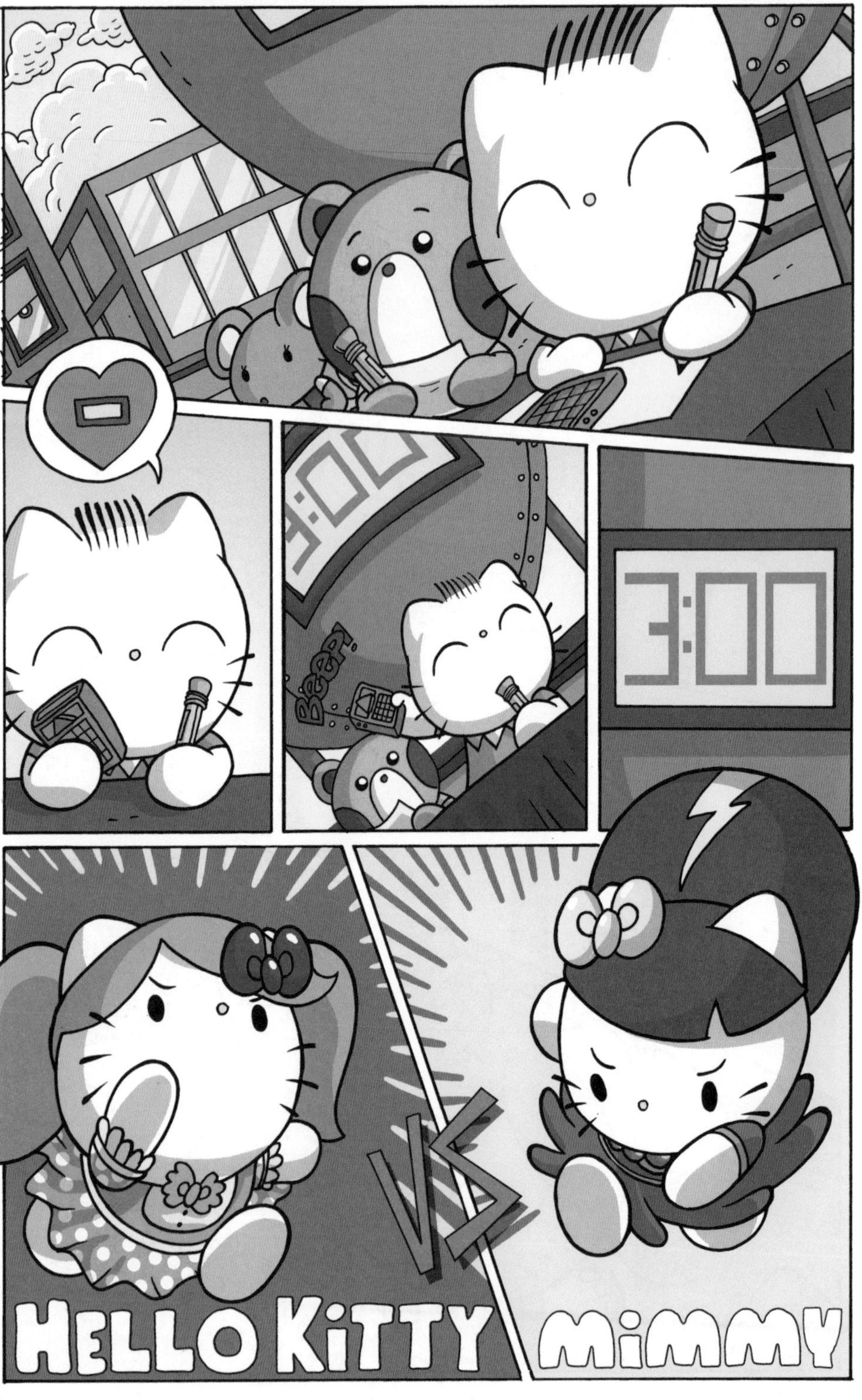
Beep!
3:00
VS
HELLO KiTTY
MiMMY

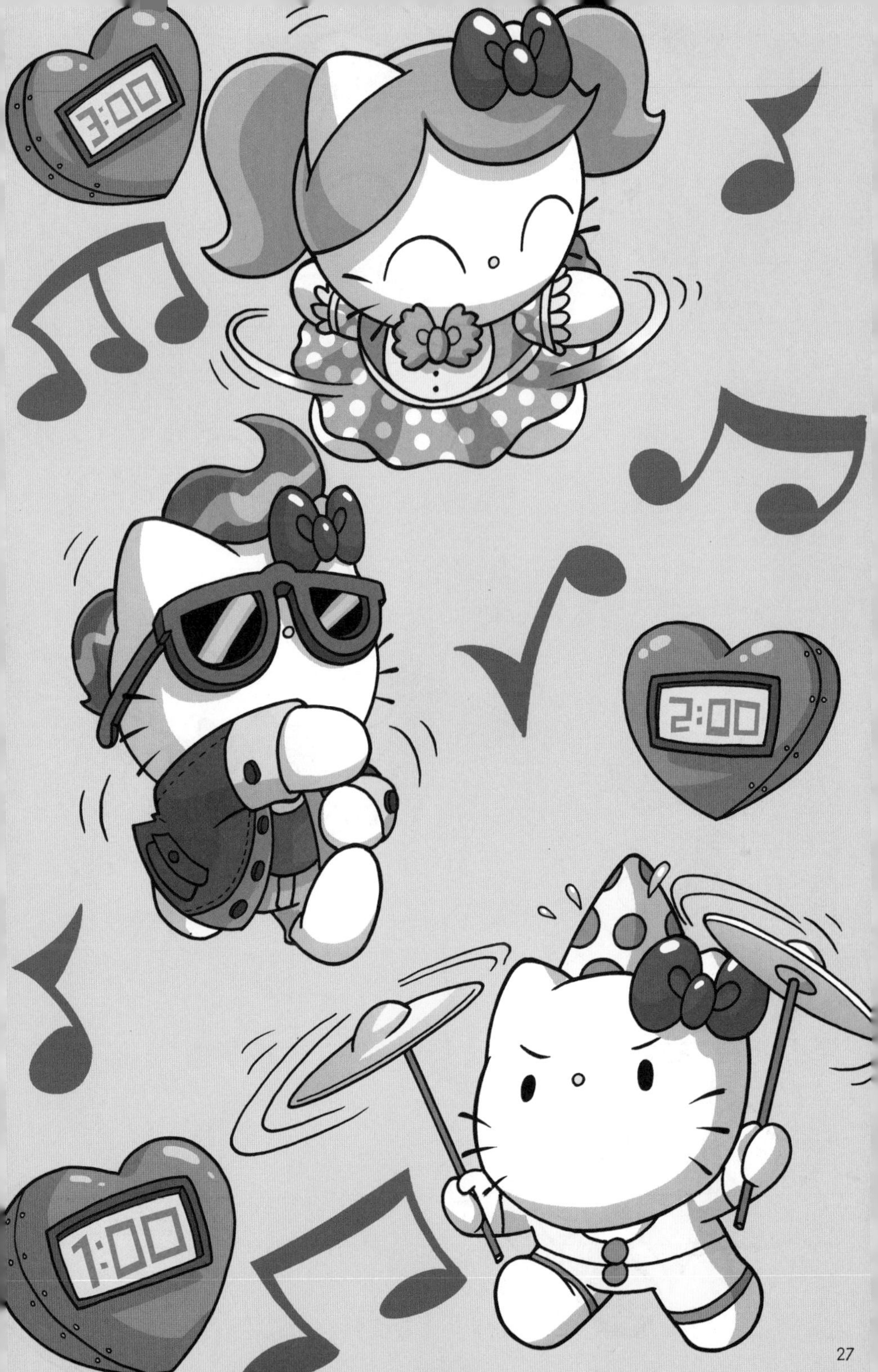
3:00
2:00
1:00

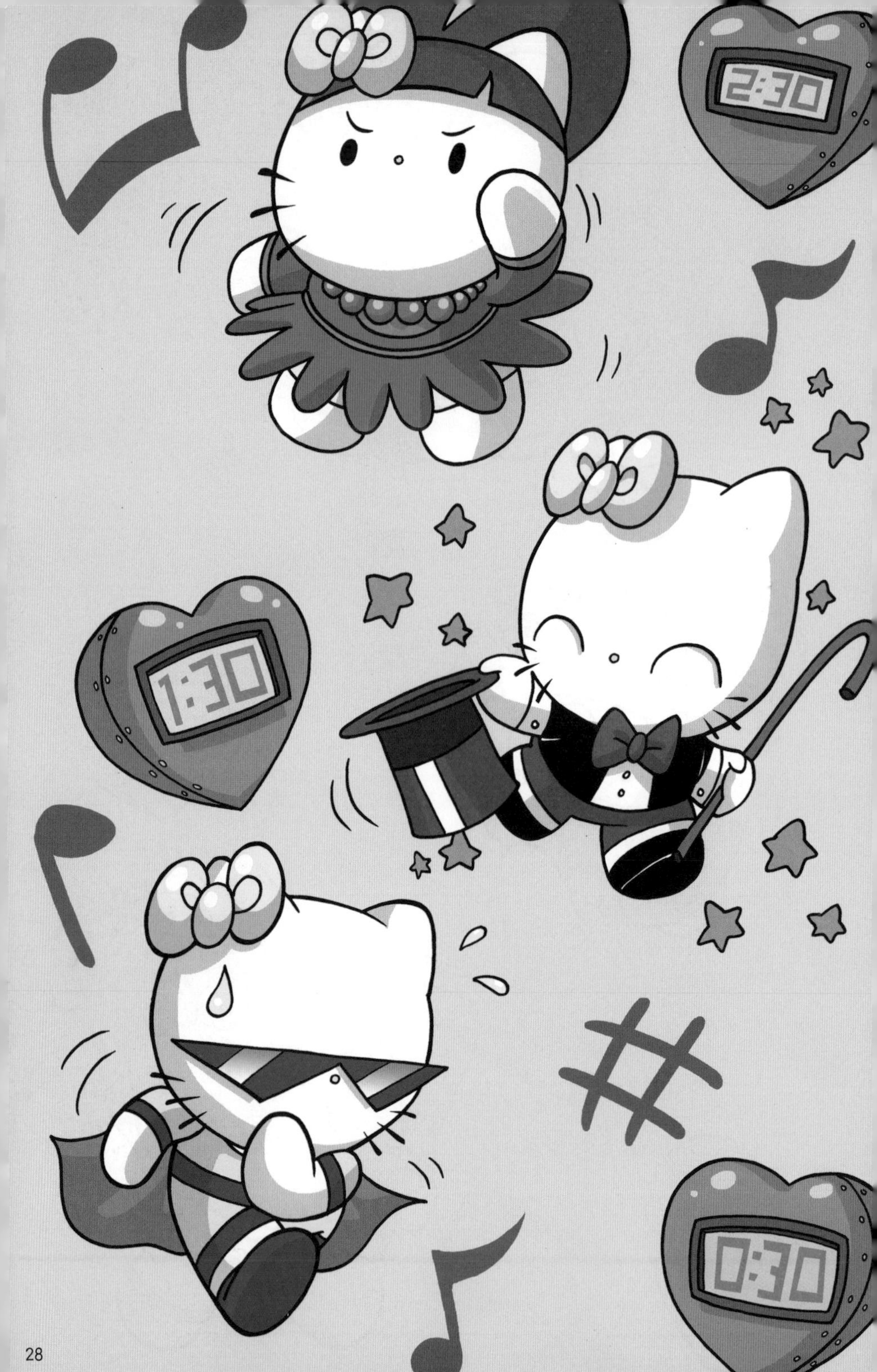
2:30
1:30
0:30

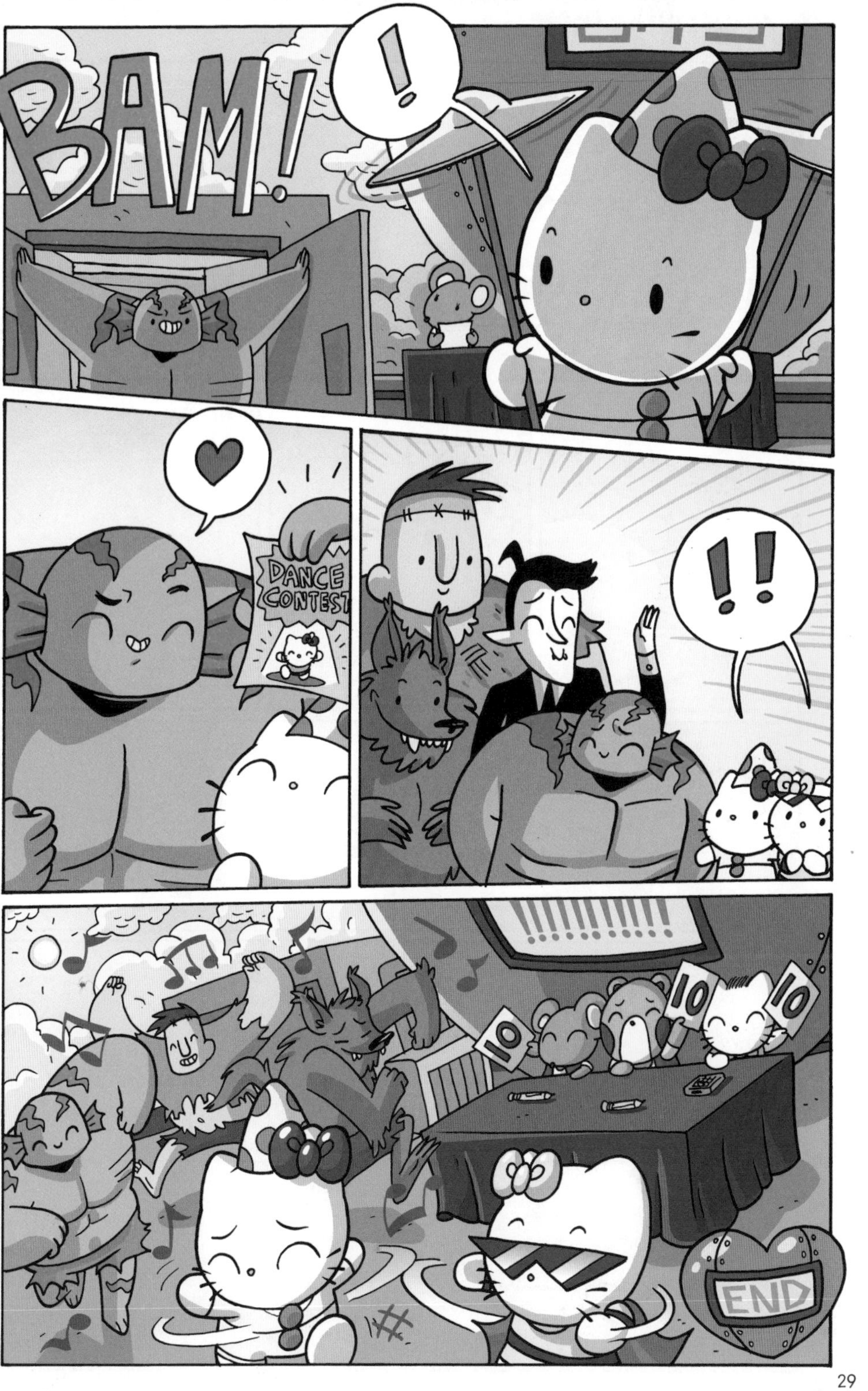
BAM!
!
DANCE CONTEST
!!
!!!!!!!!!!!
10
10
10
END

MIX TAPE

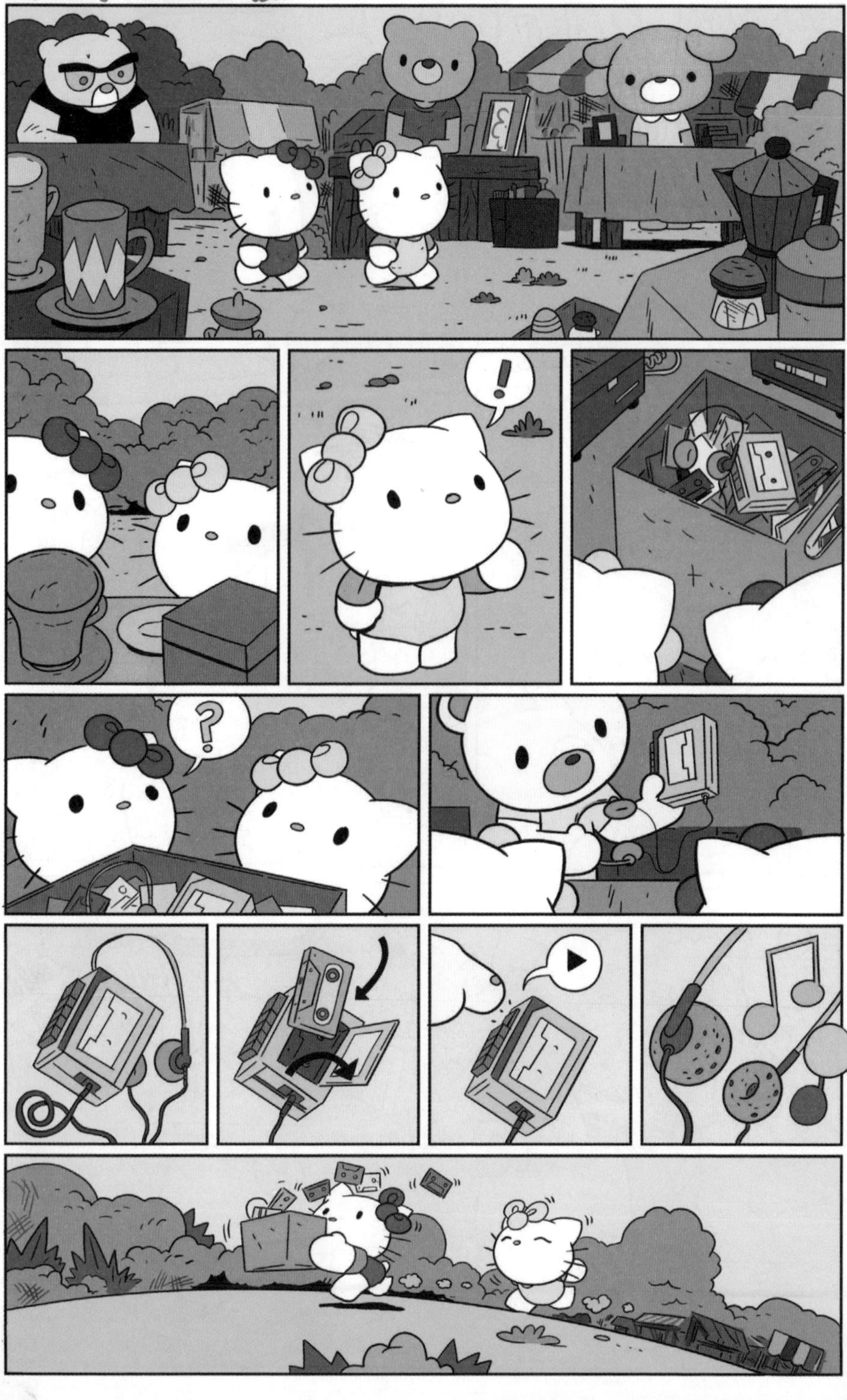
!
?

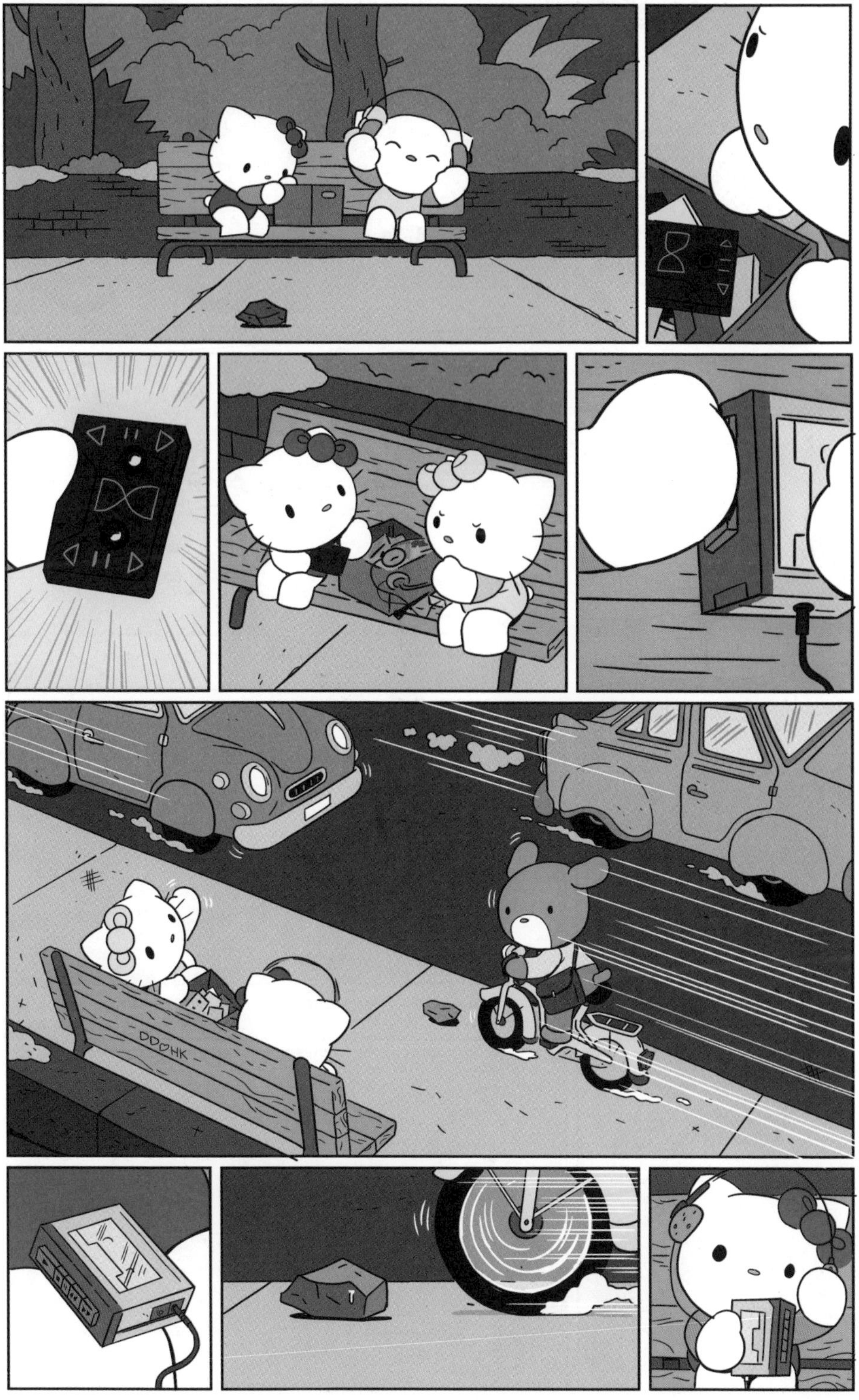
DD♡HK

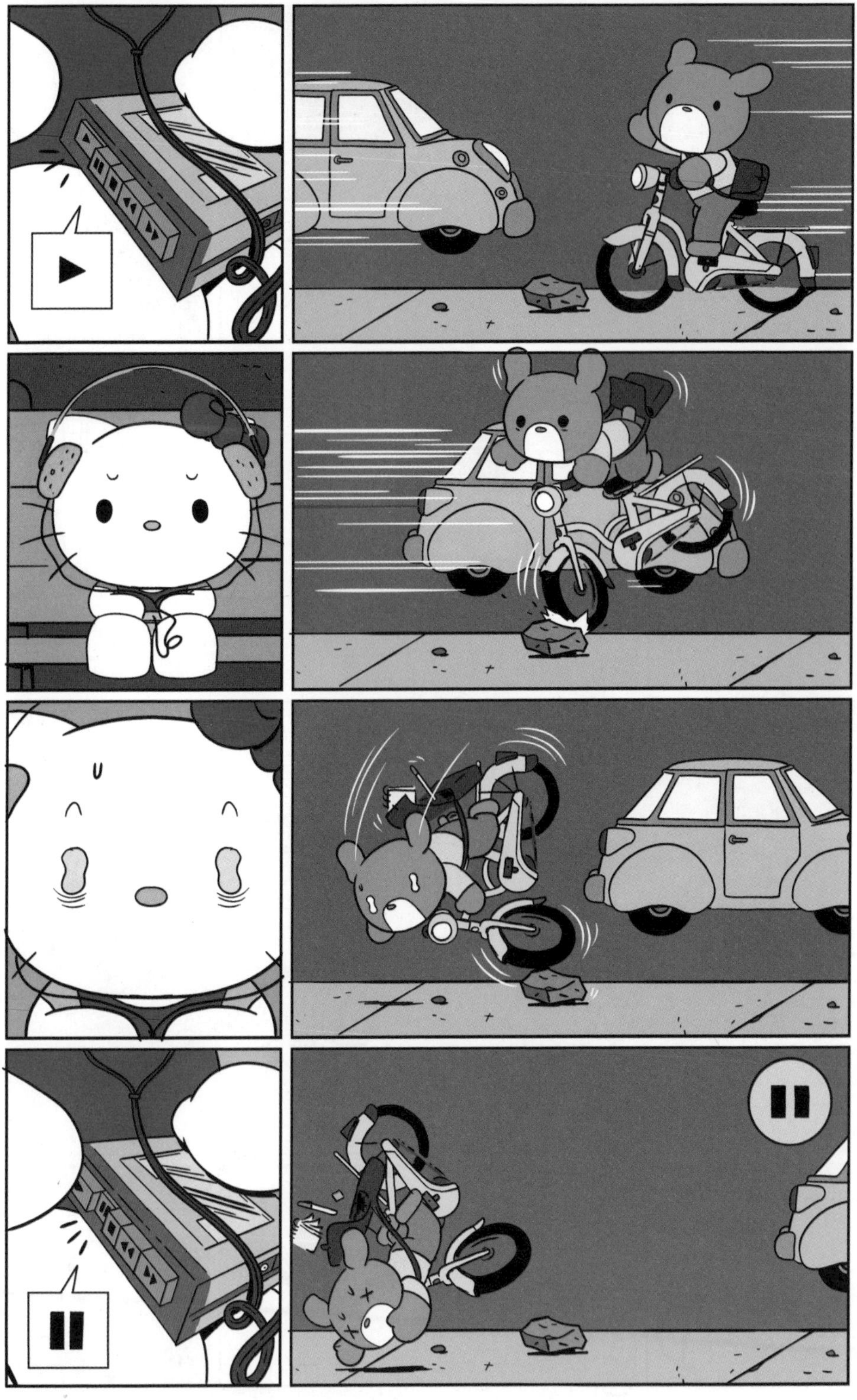

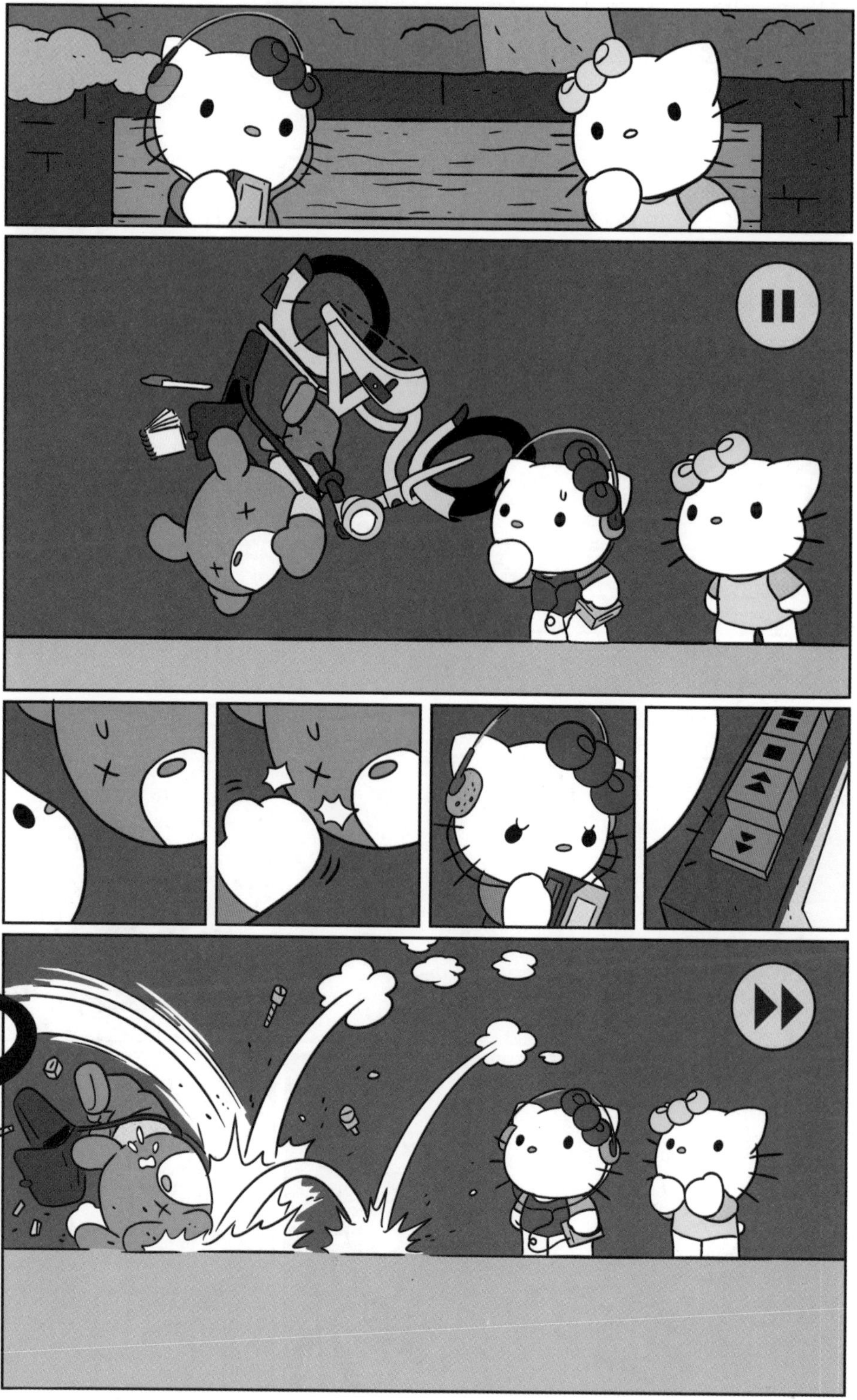

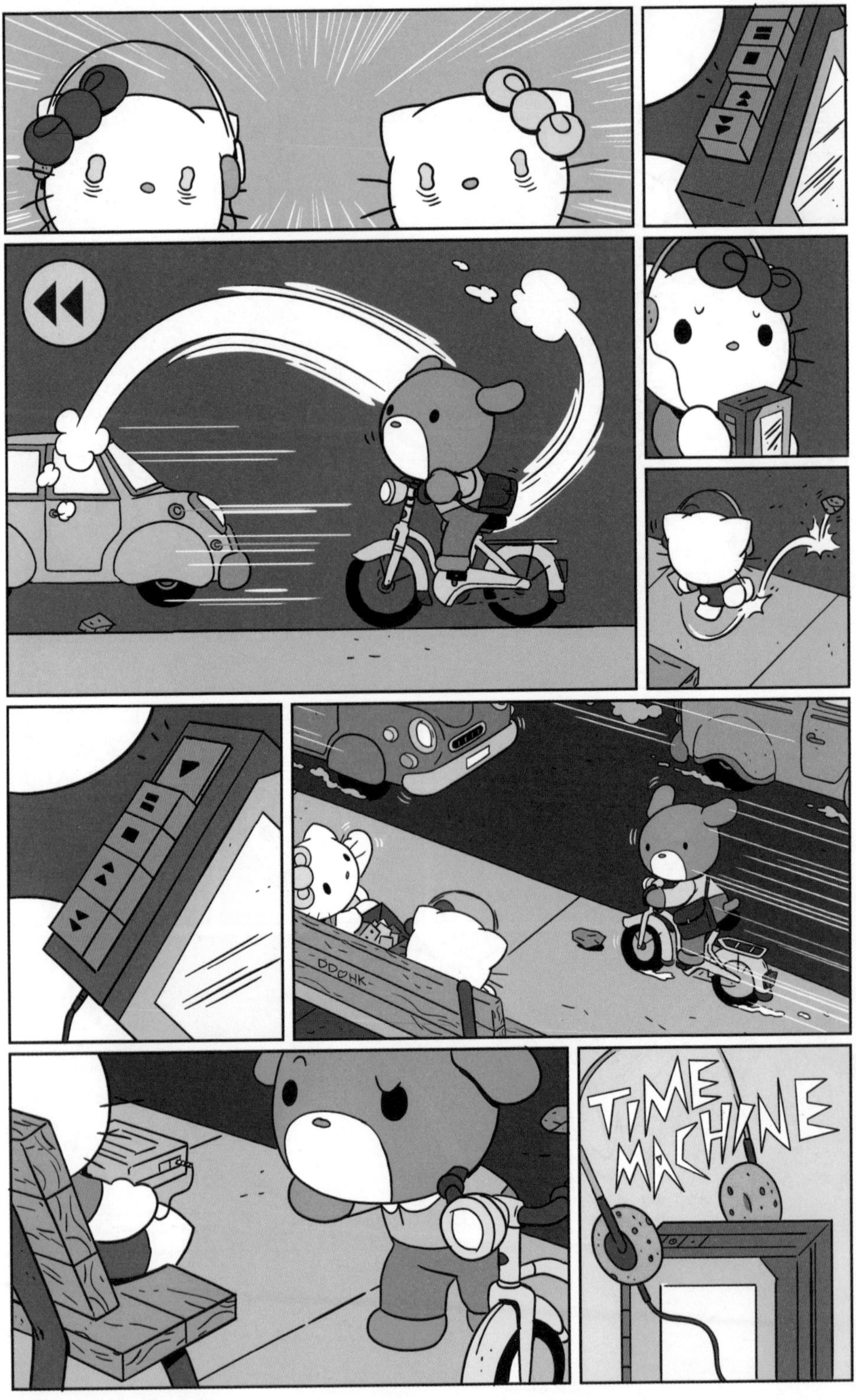
DD♡HK
TIME MACHINE

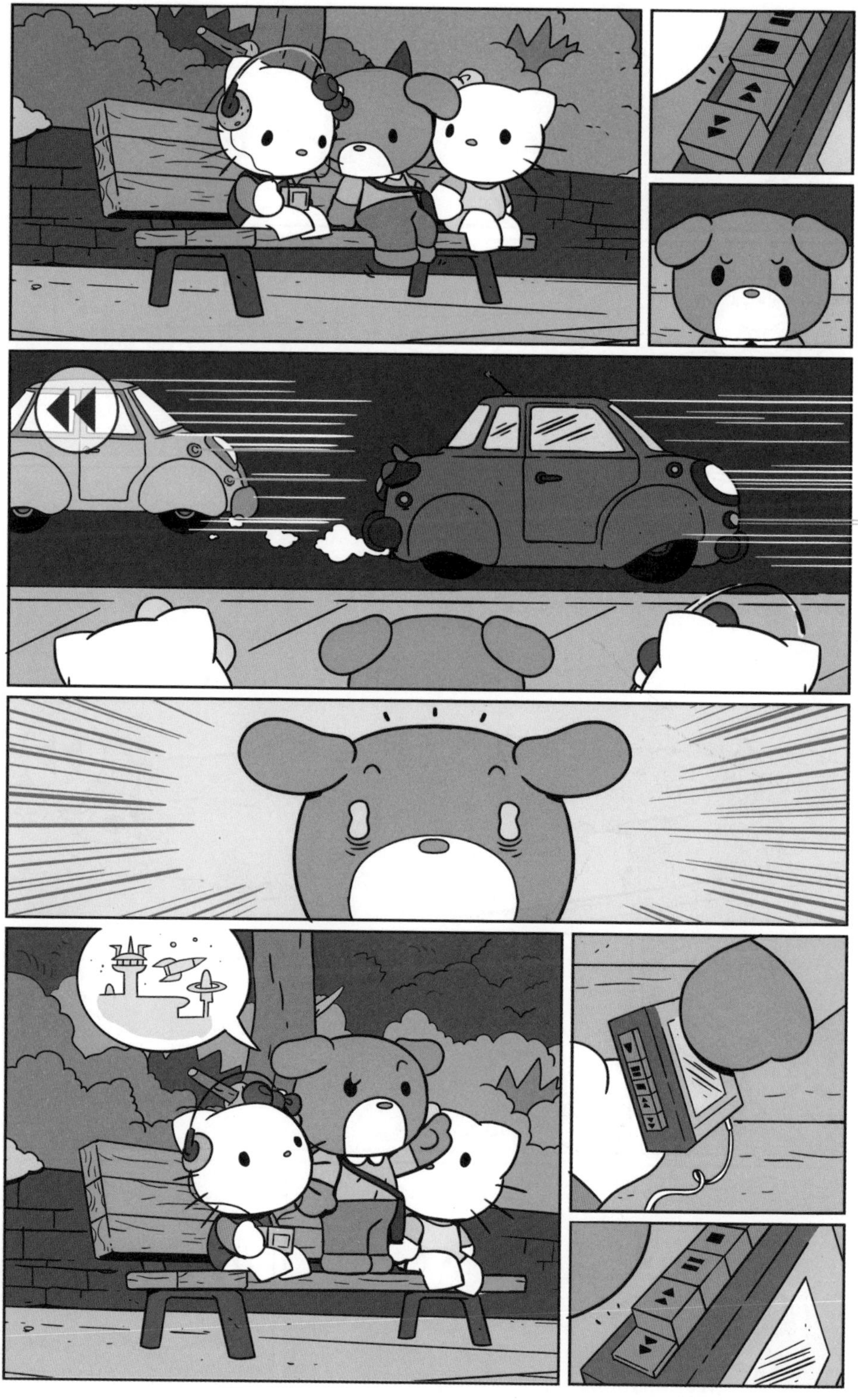

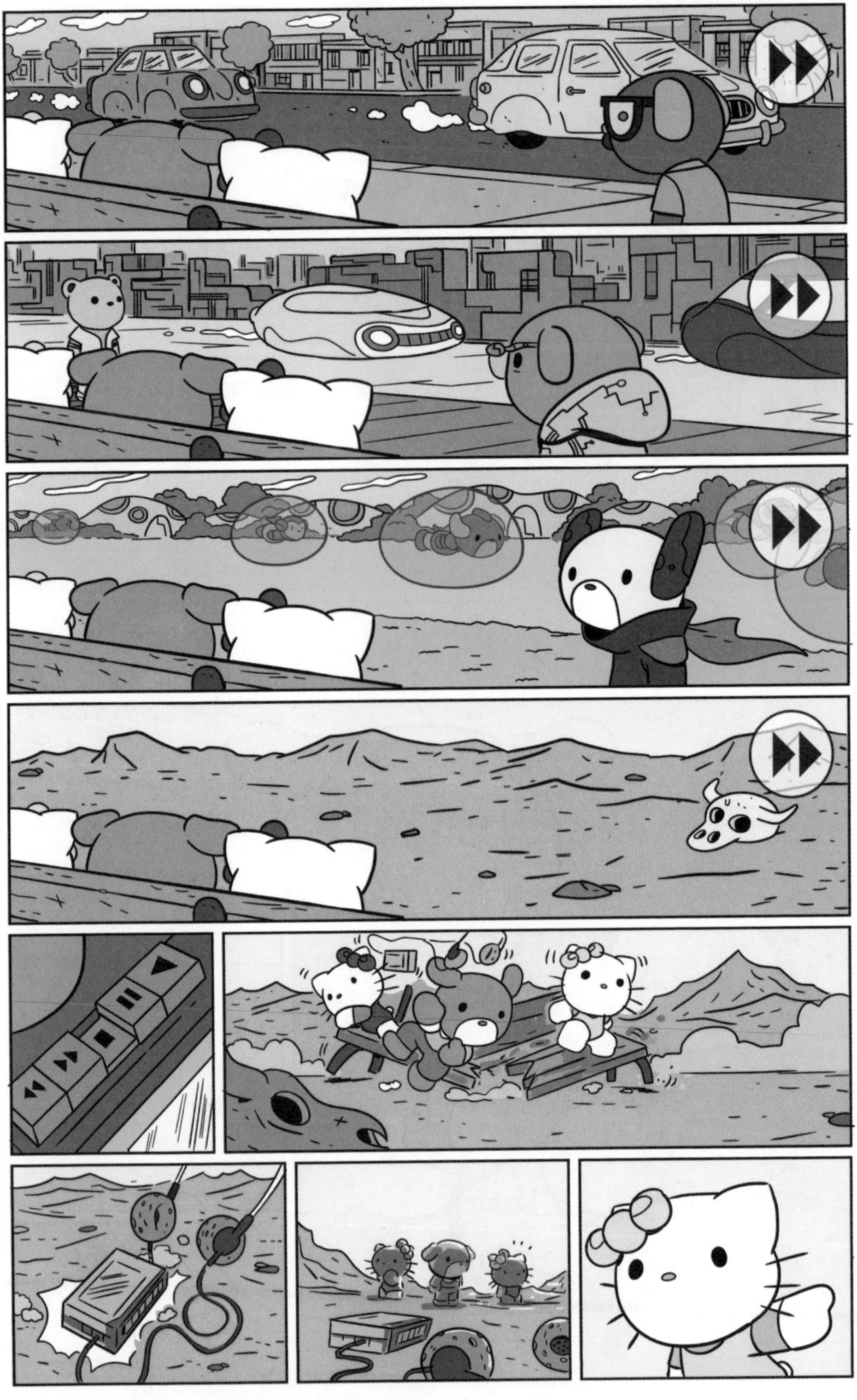

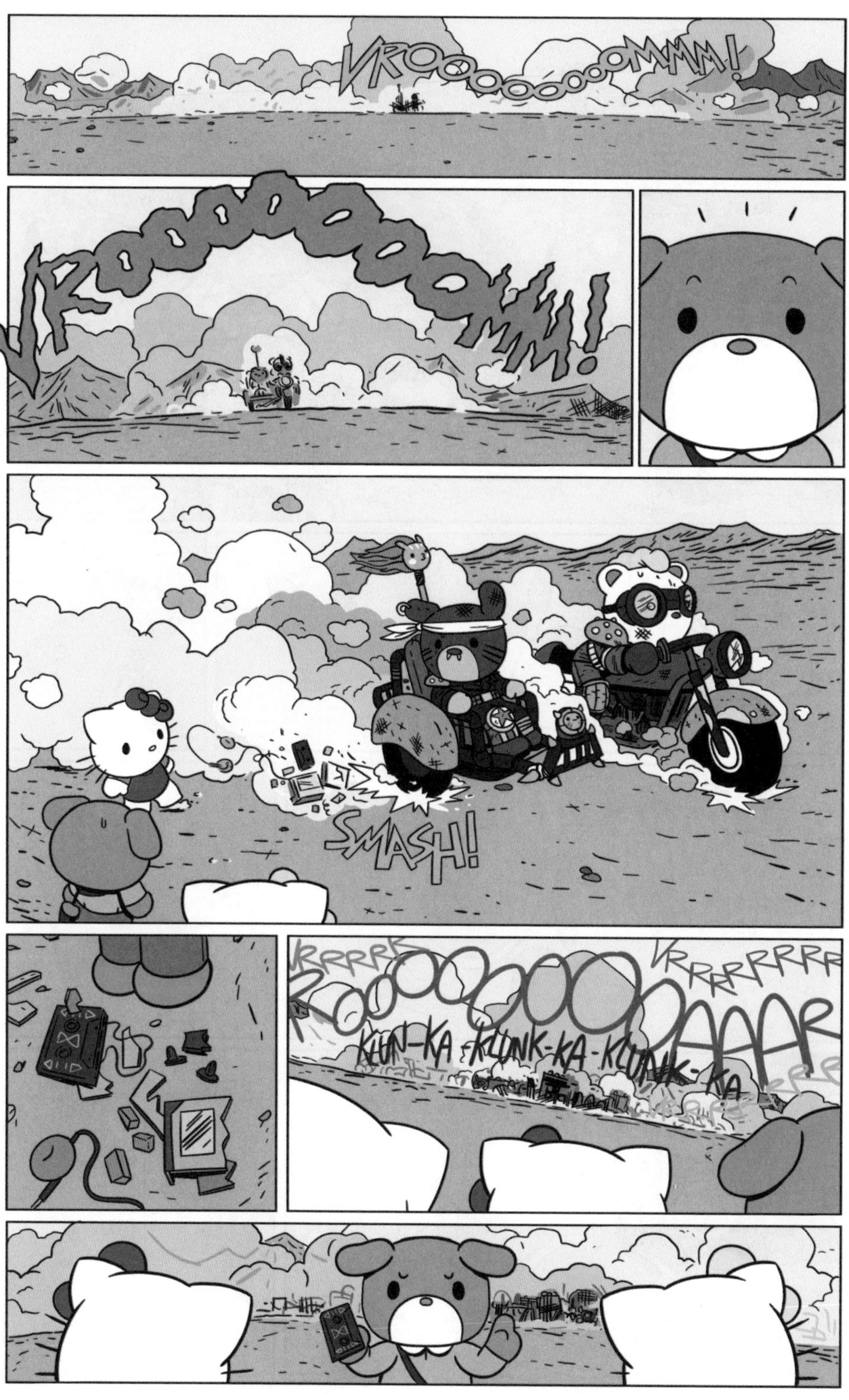
VROOOOOOOOOMMMM!
VROOOOOOOOOMMM!
SMASH!
VRRRRR
ROOOOOOOOAAAAR
VRRRRRRRRR
KLUNK-KA-KLUNK-KA-KLUNK-KA

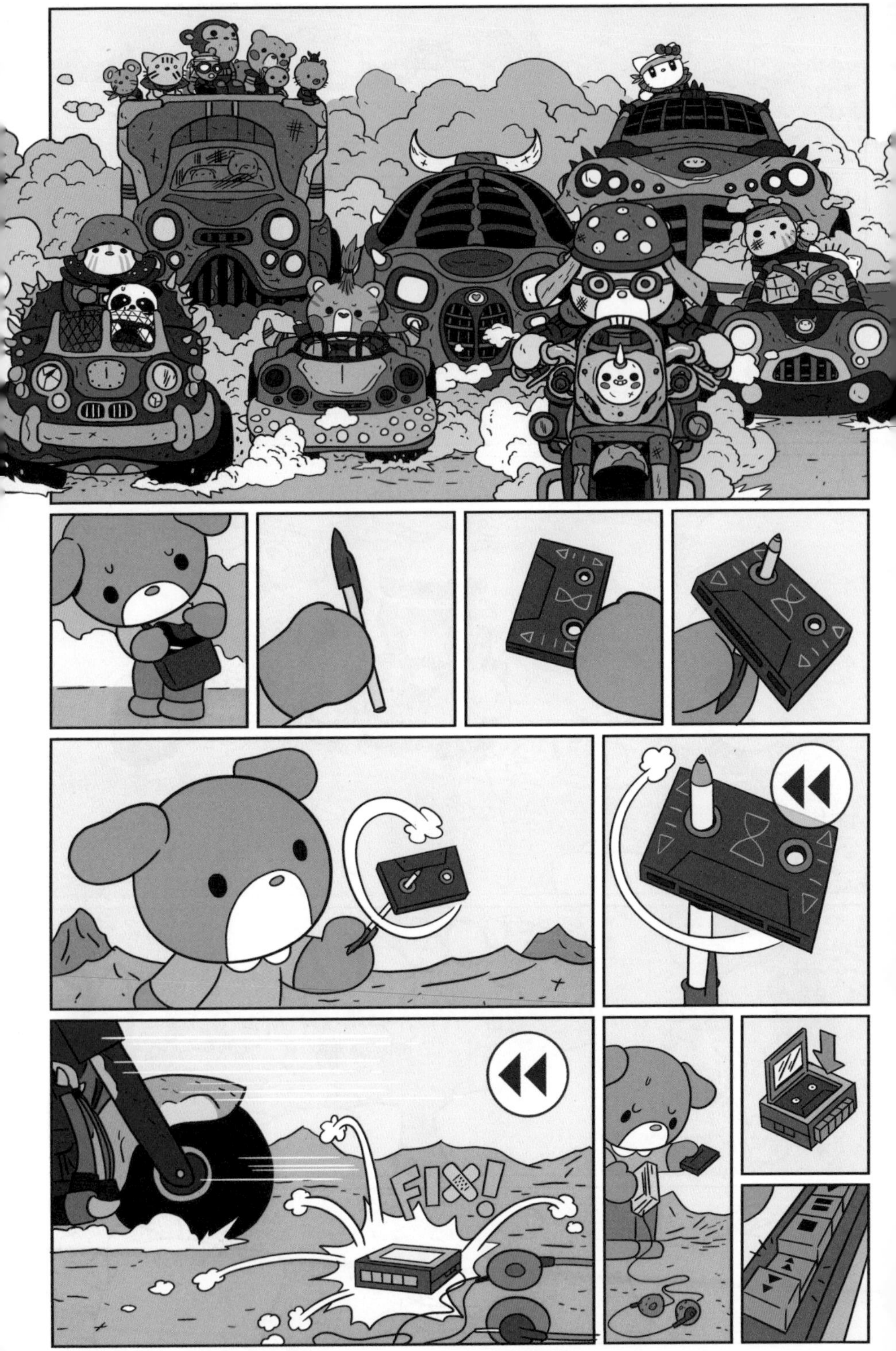
FIX!

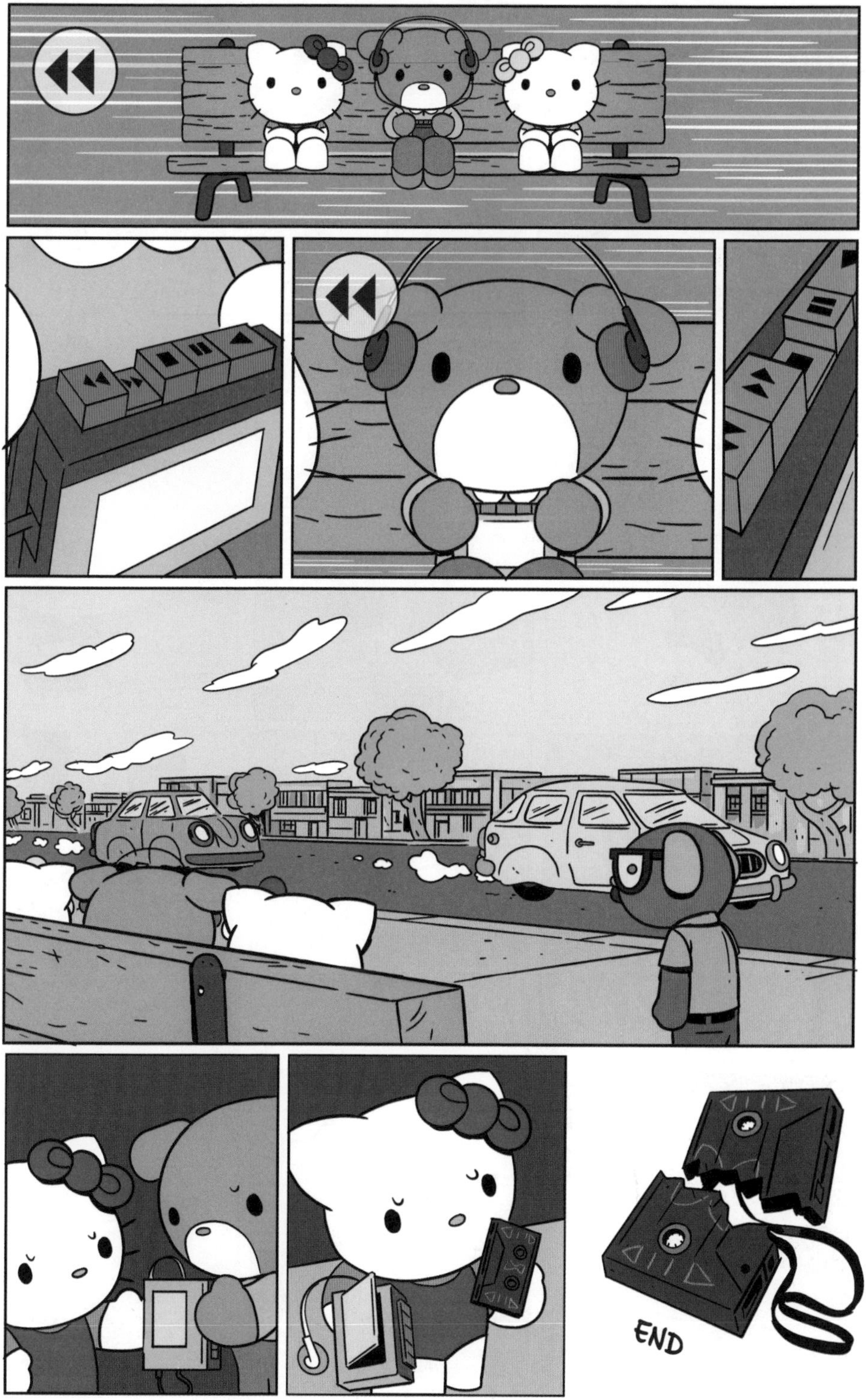
END

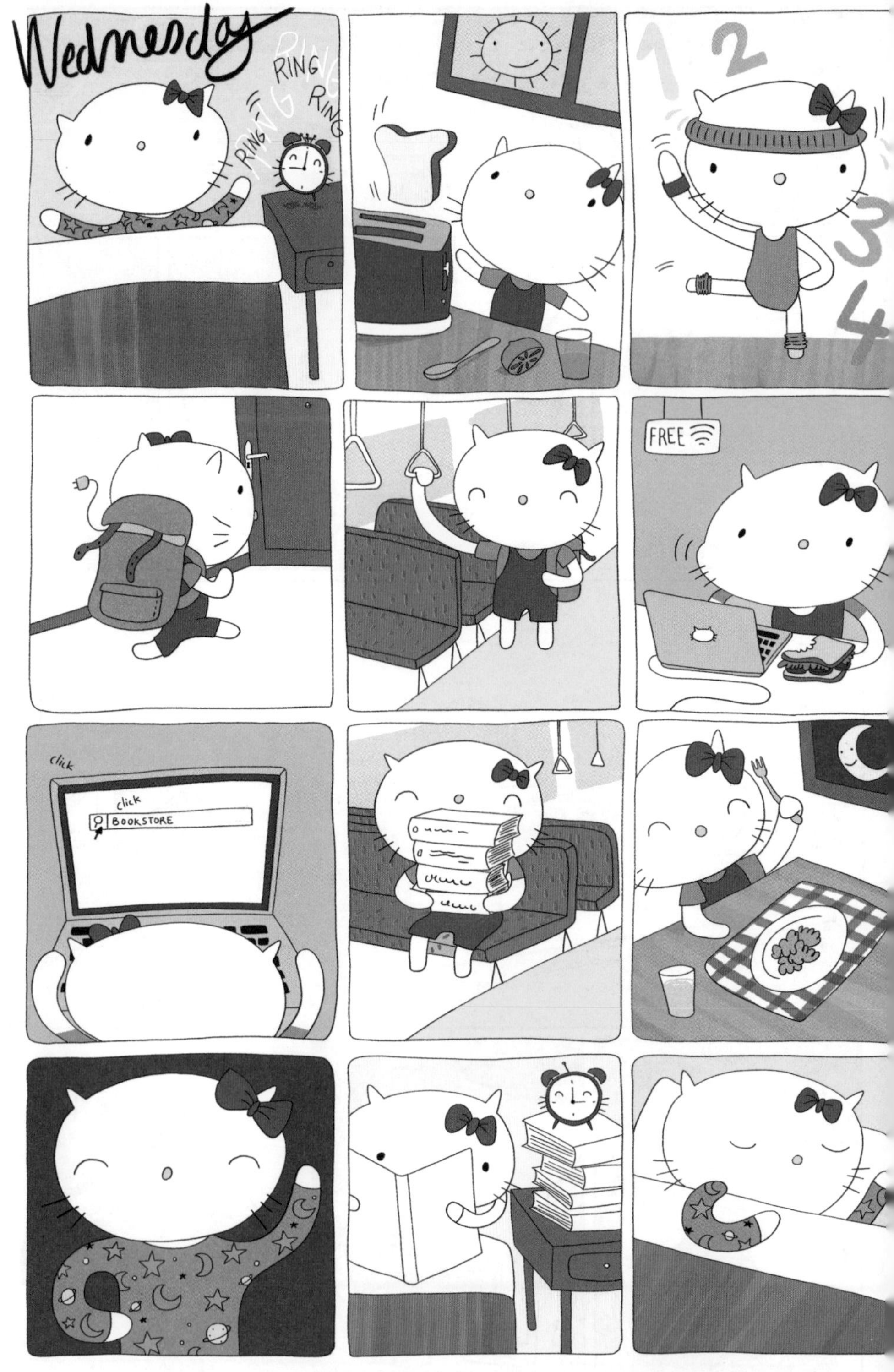
Wednesday
RING
RING
RING
RING
1
2
3
4
FREE
click
click
BOOKSTORE

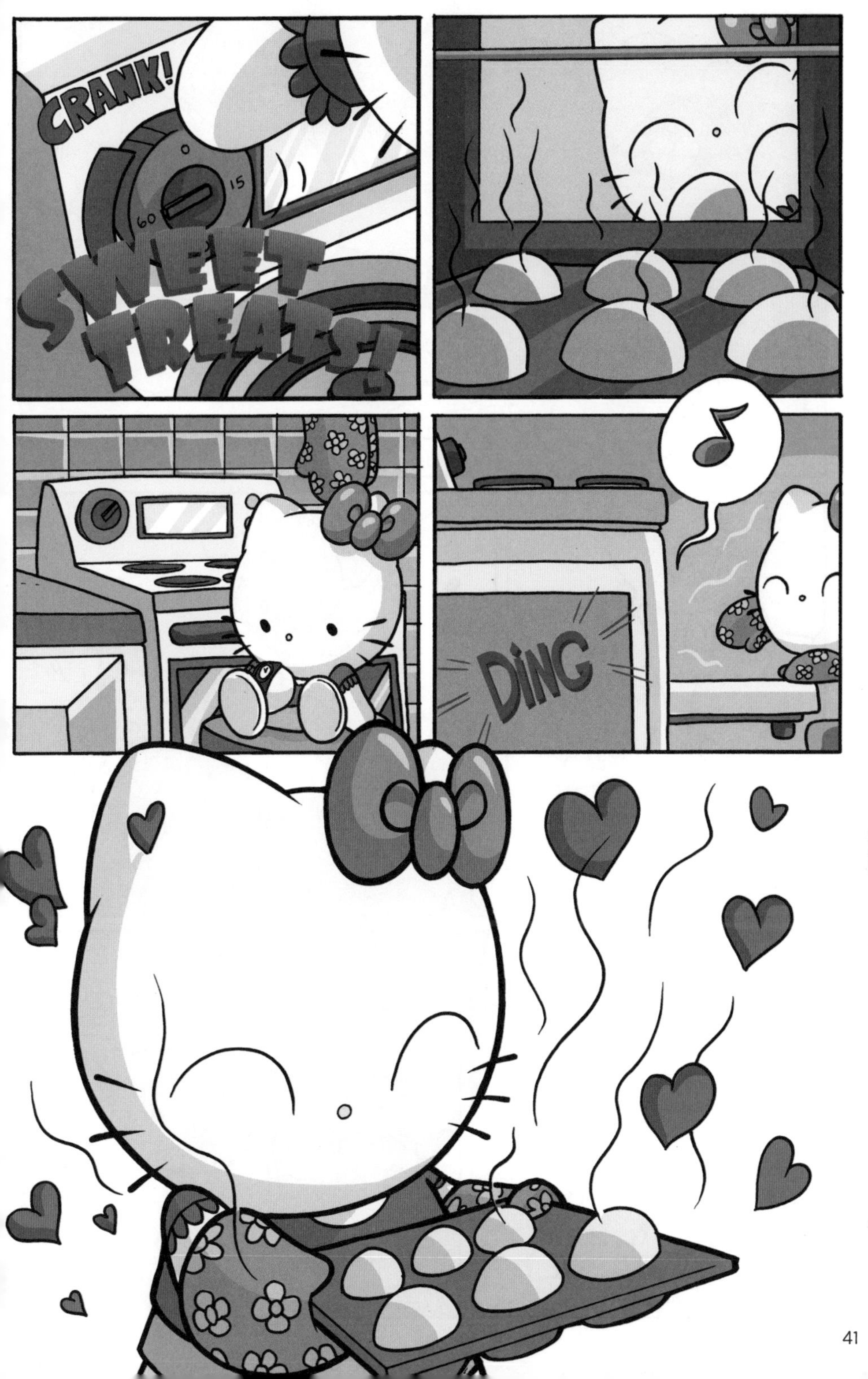
CRANK!
0
15
60
SWEET TREATS!
♪
DING

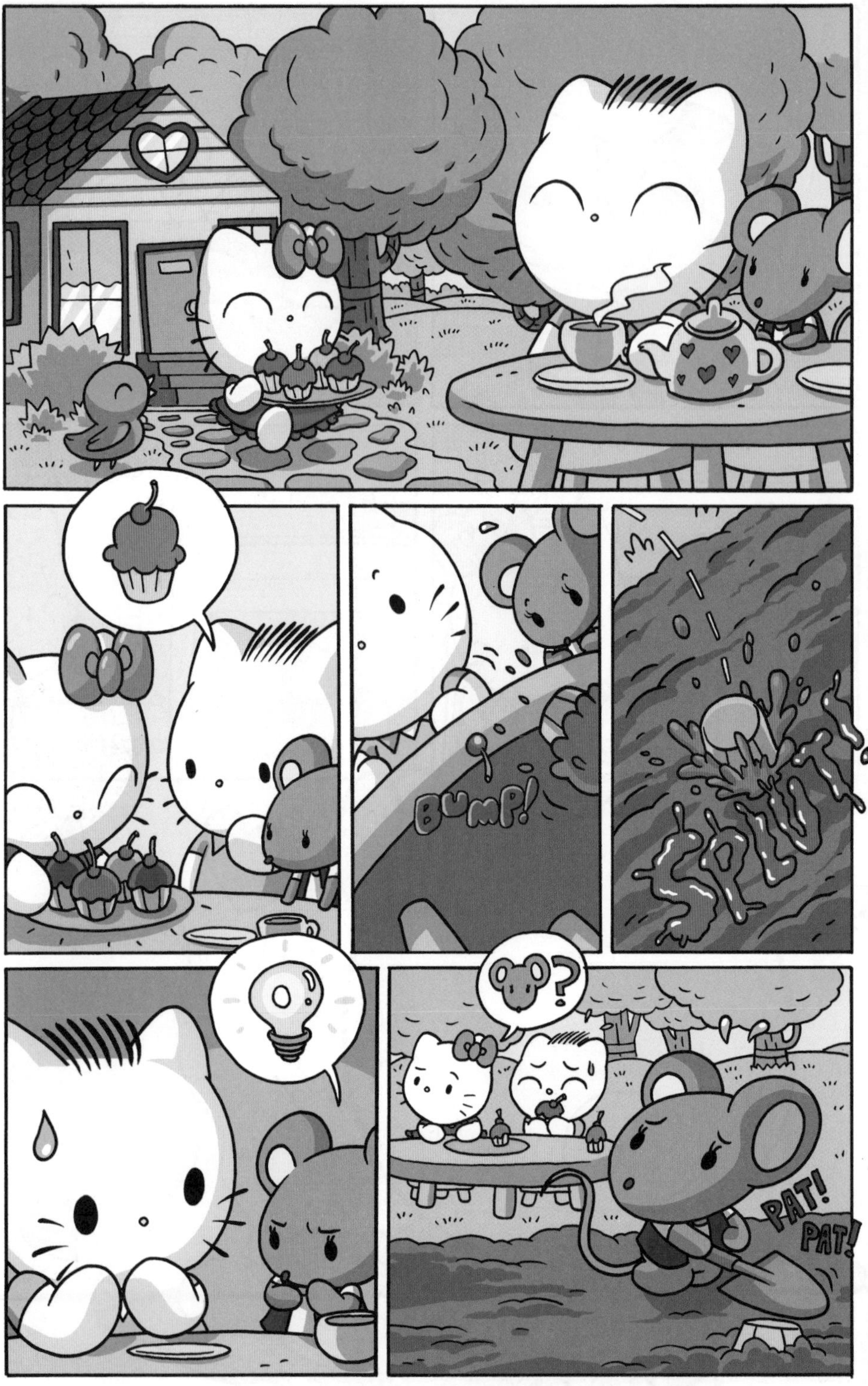
BUMP!
SPLUT!
?
PAT!
PAT!

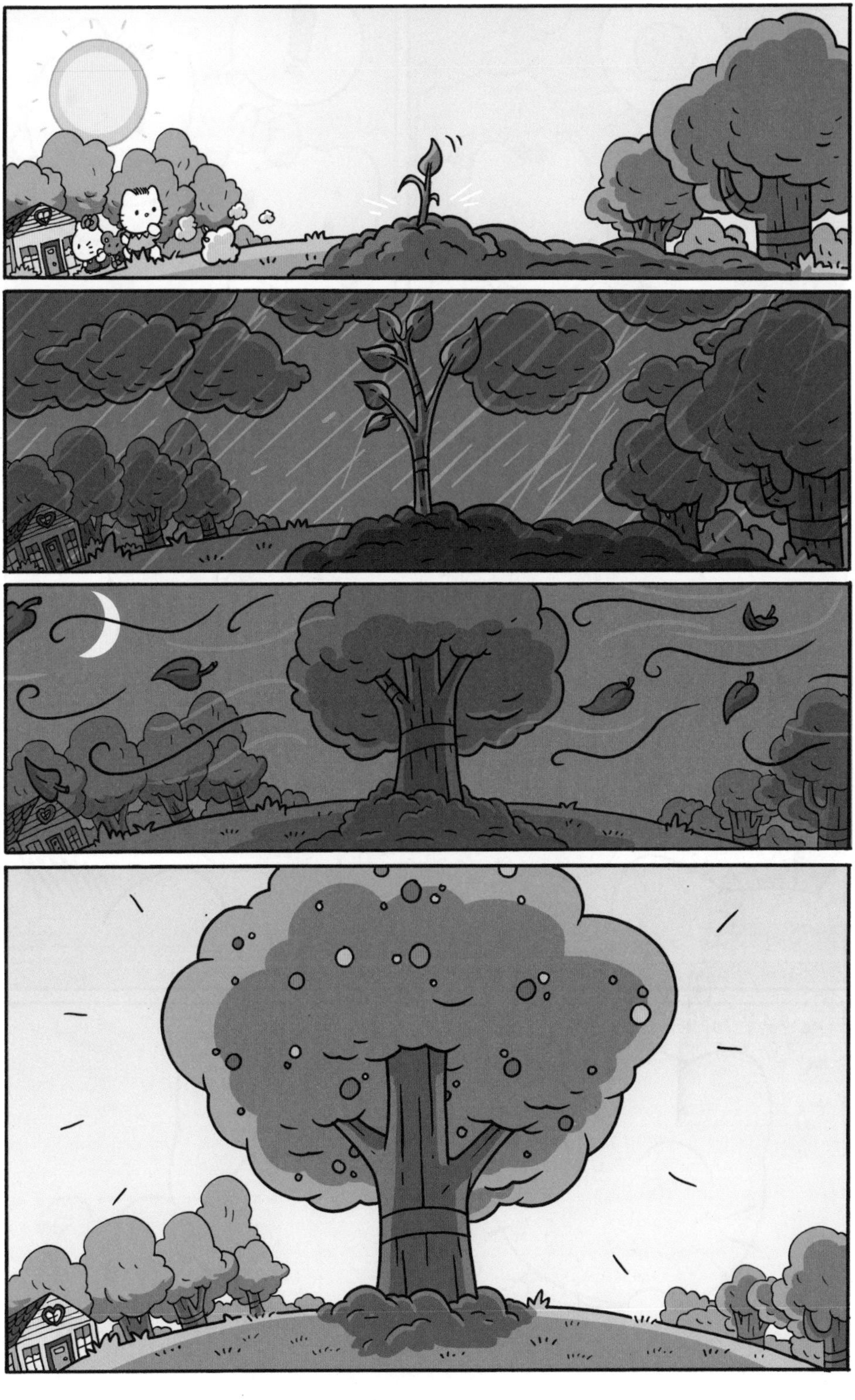

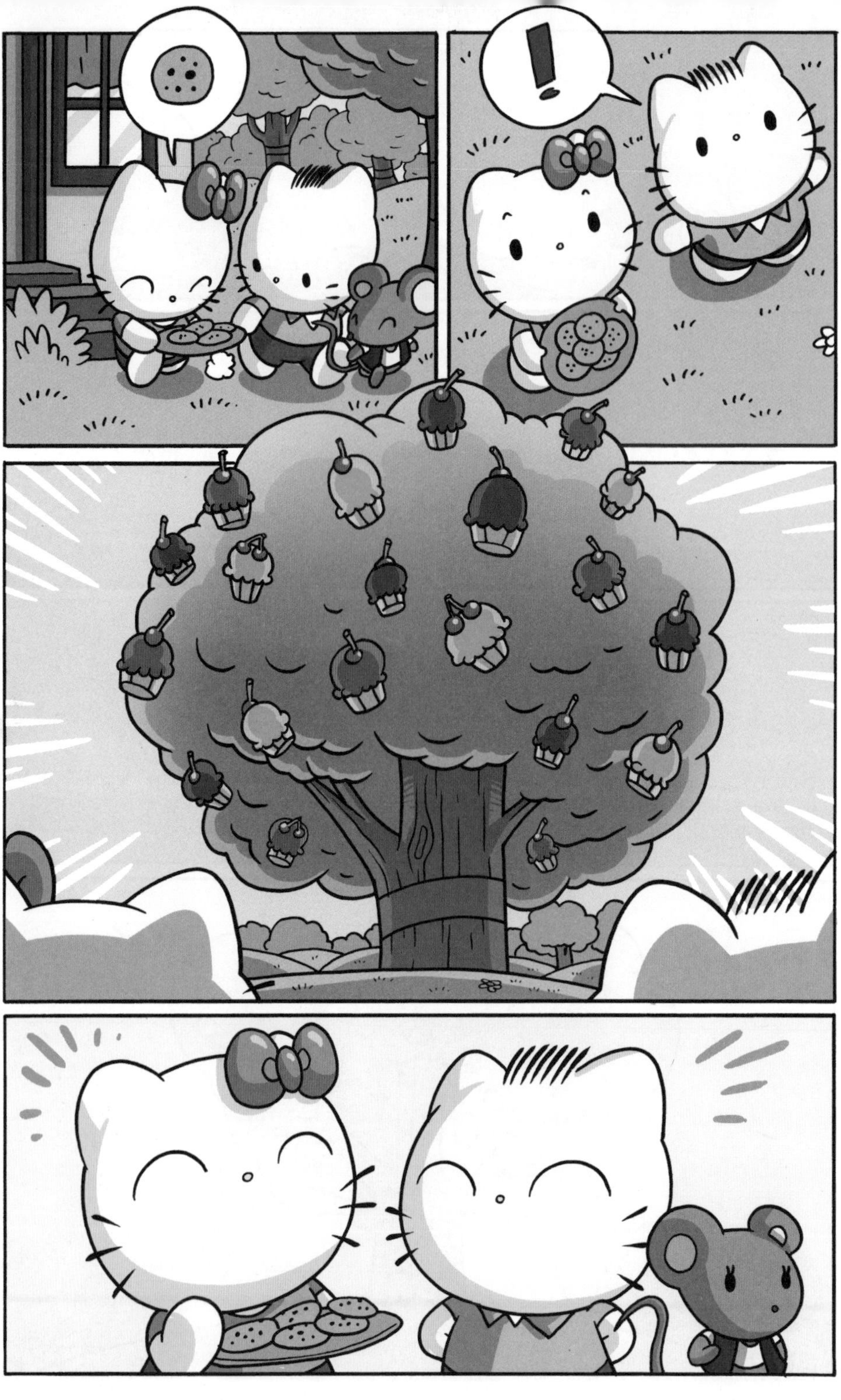
!

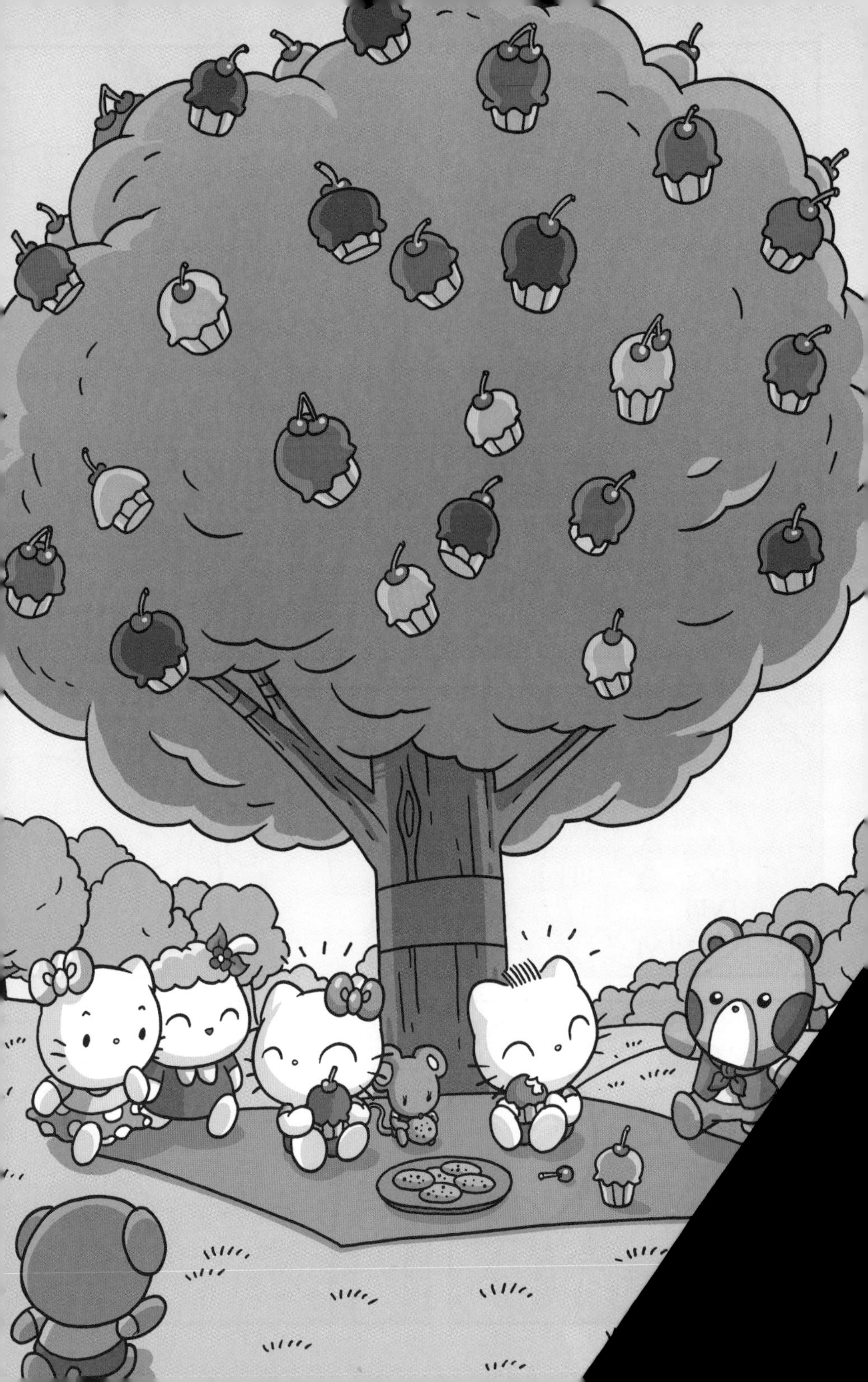

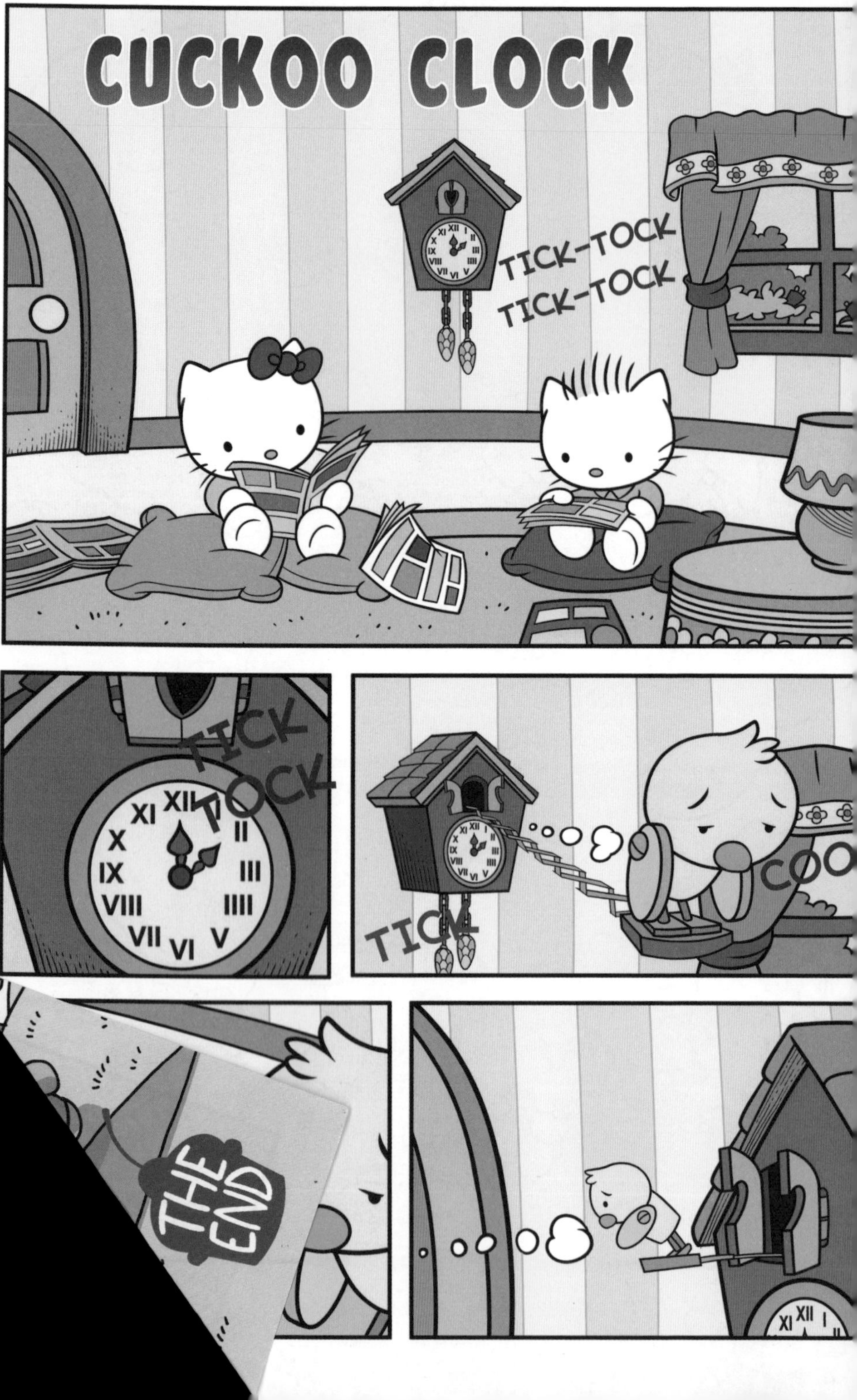
CUCKOO CLOCK
TICK-TOCK
TICK-TOCK
TICK
TOCK
TICK
COO
THE END

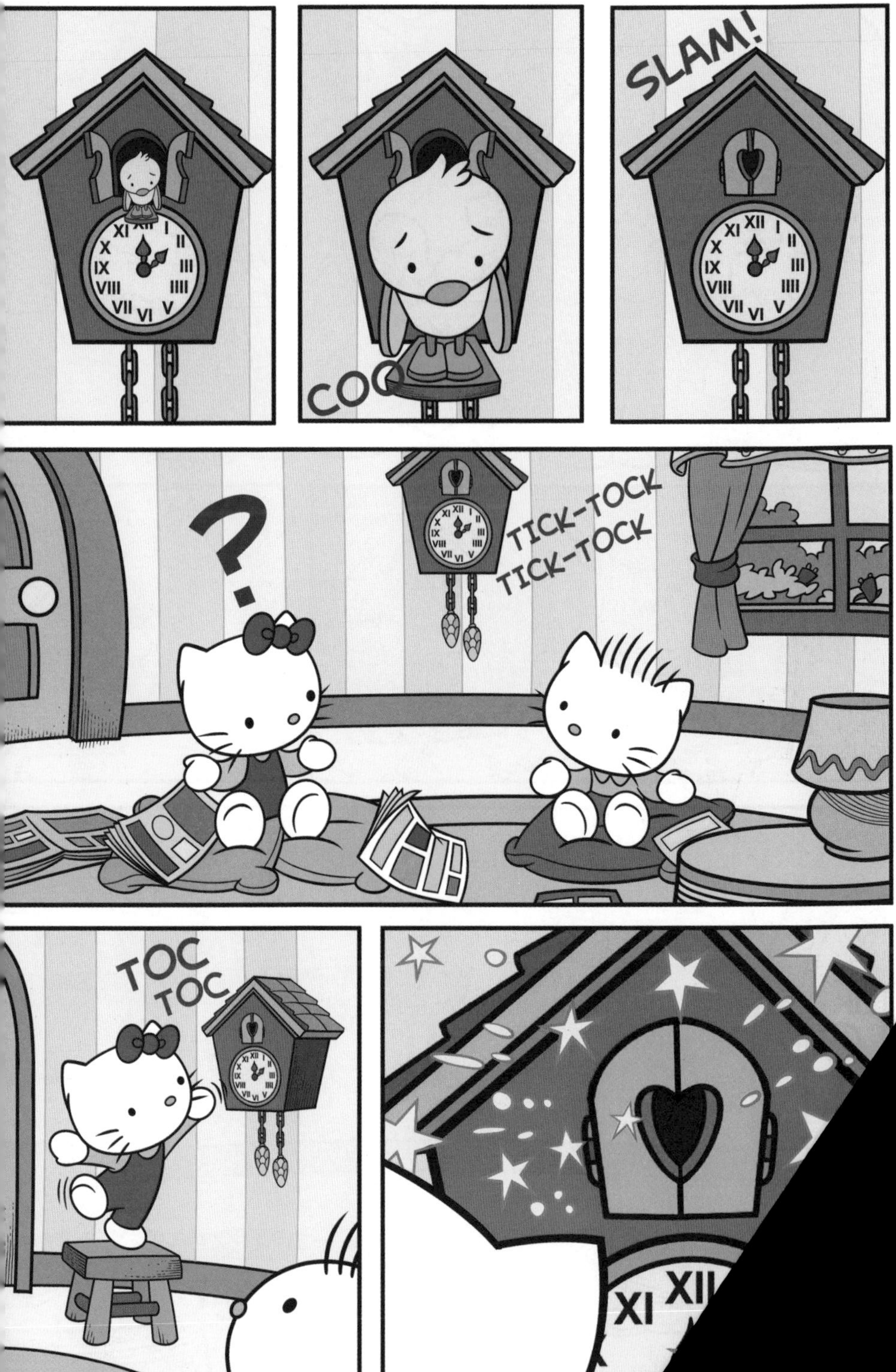
COO
SLAM!
TICK-TOCK
TICK-TOCK
TOC
TOC

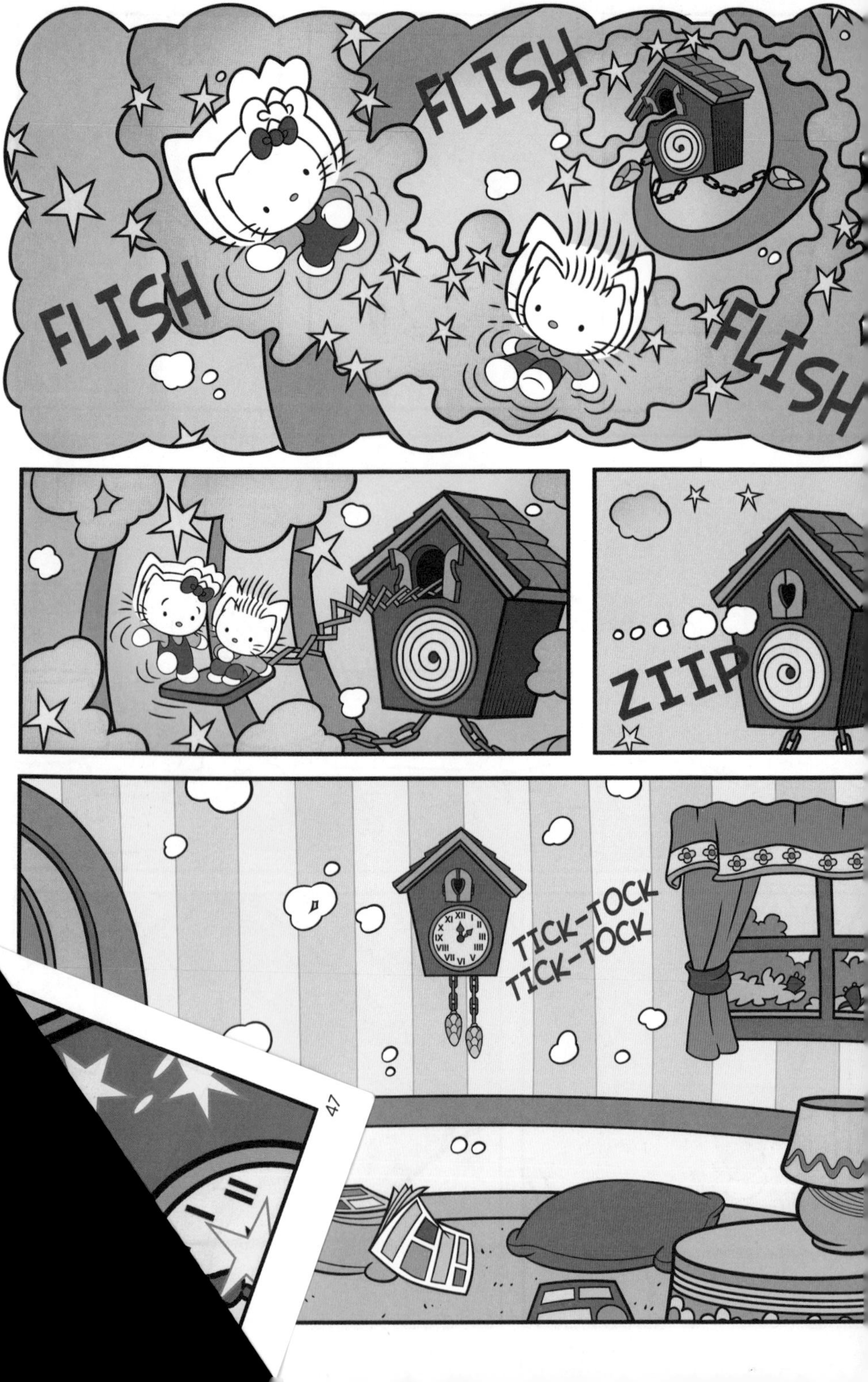

FLISH
FLISH
FLISH
ZIIP
TICK-TOCK
TICK-TOCK

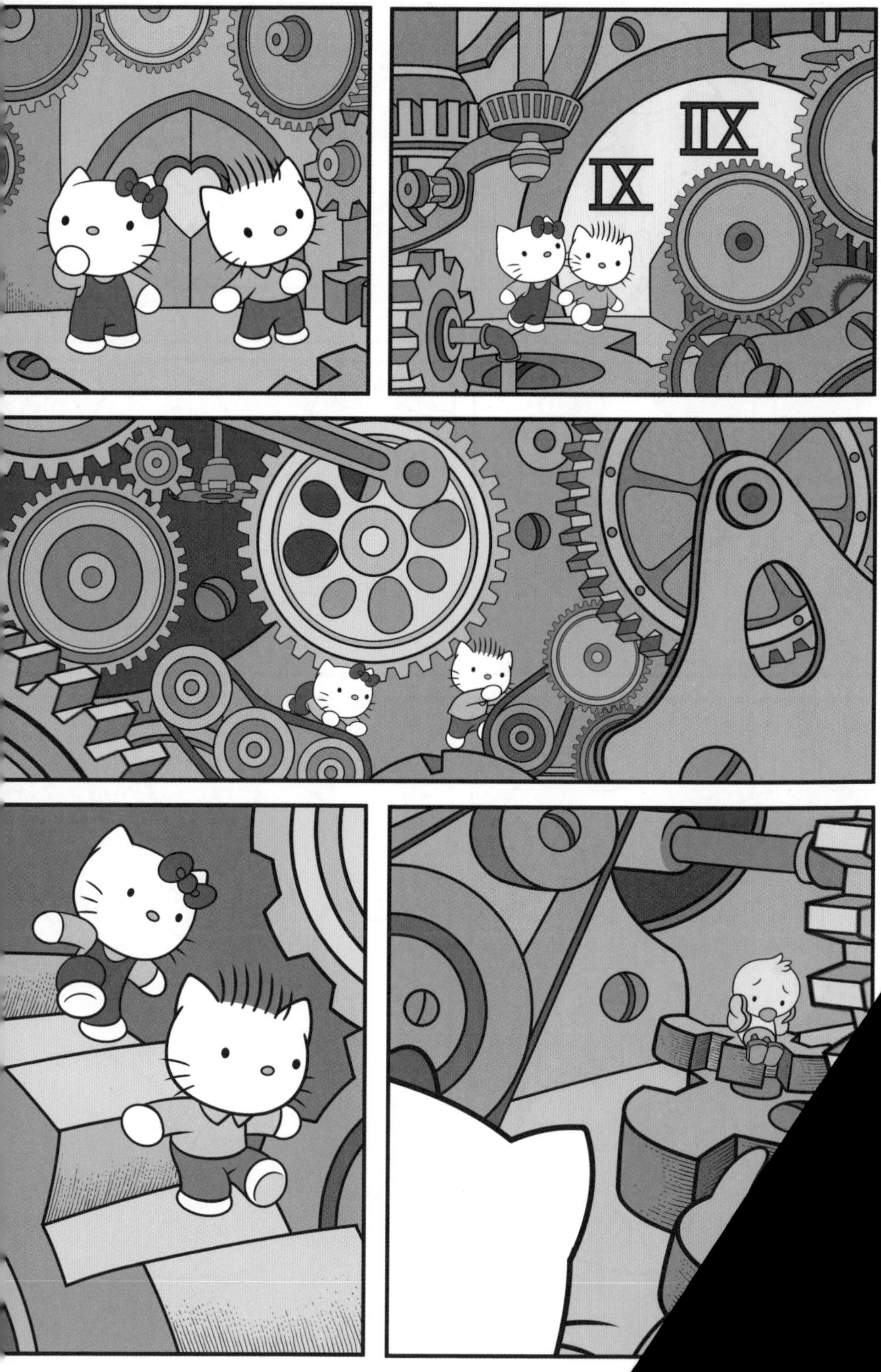
IIX
IX

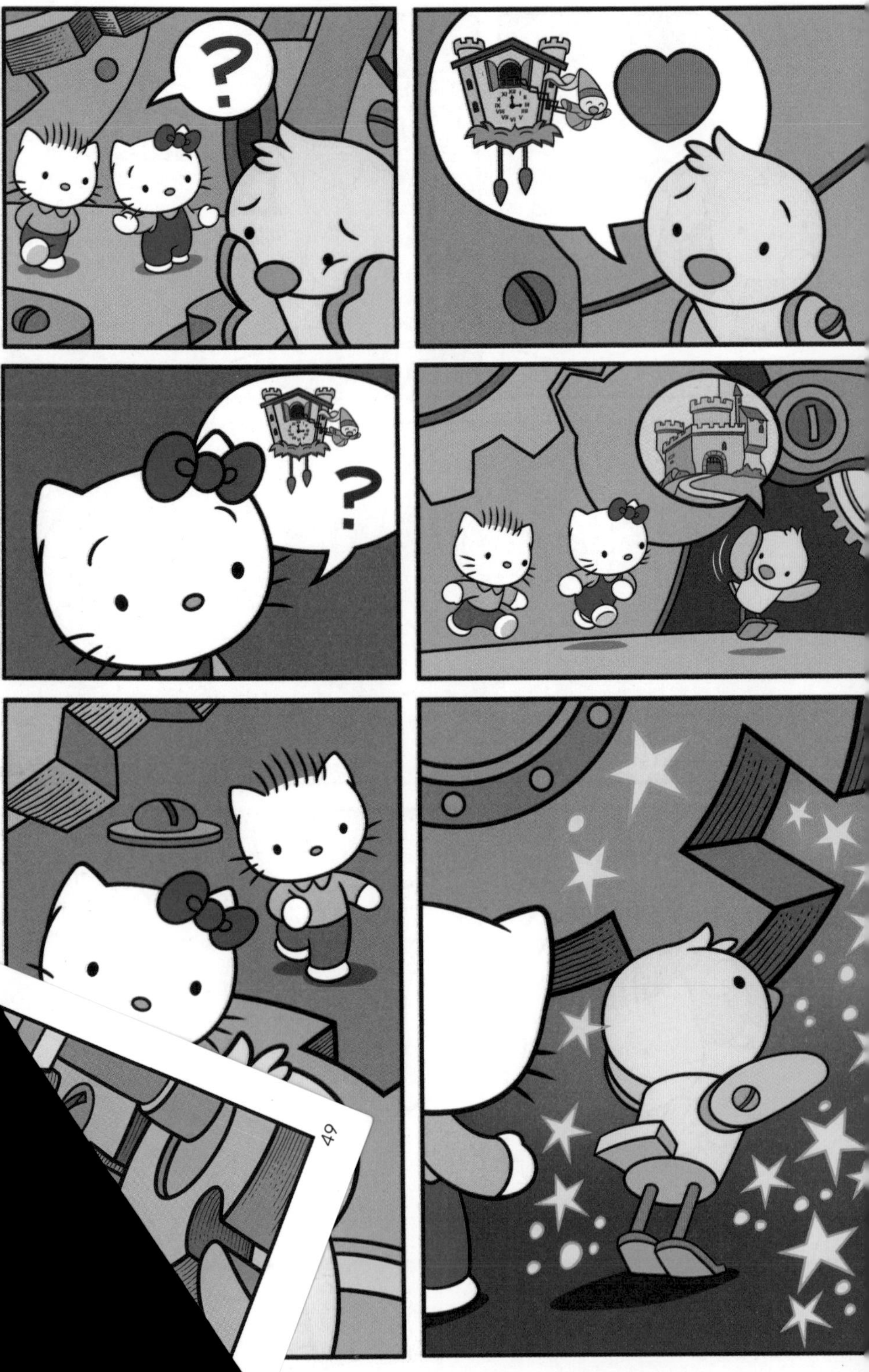
?
?

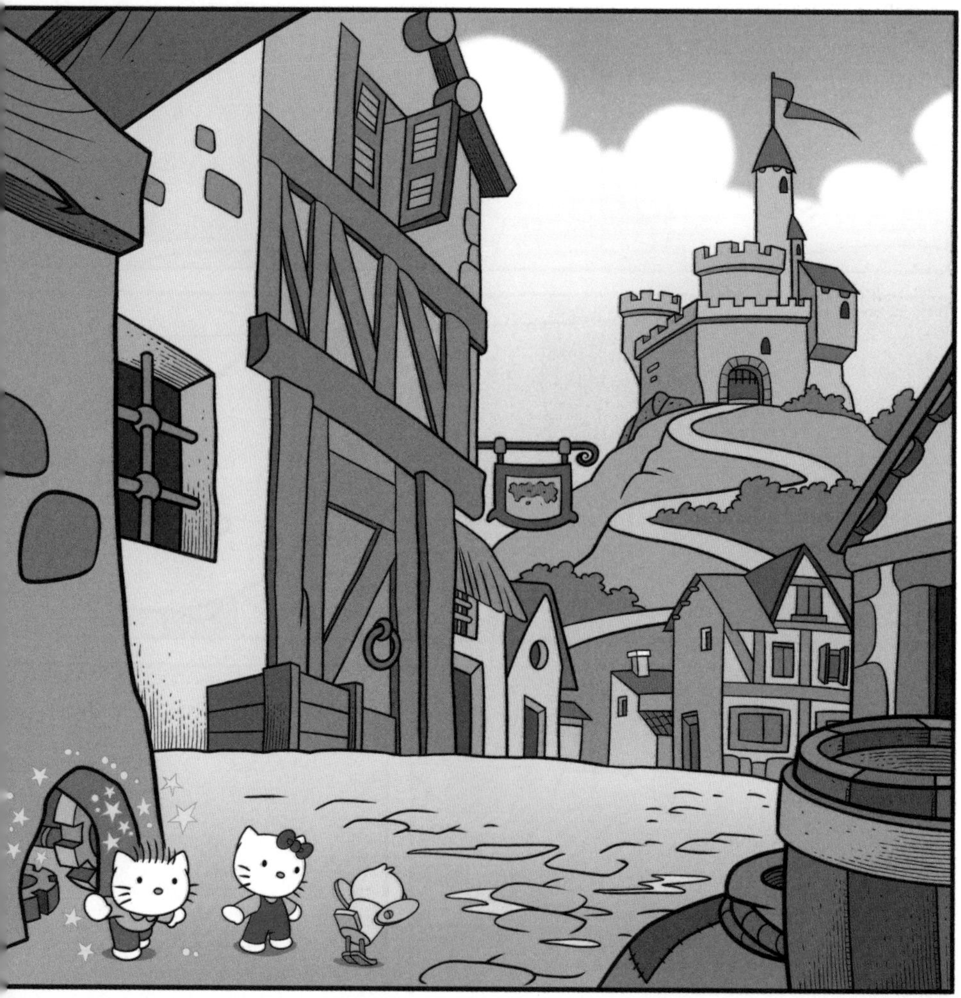

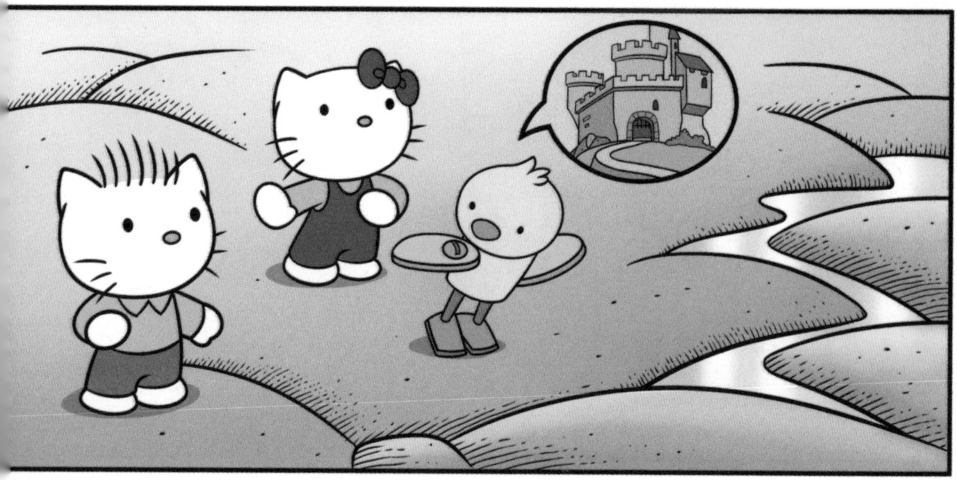

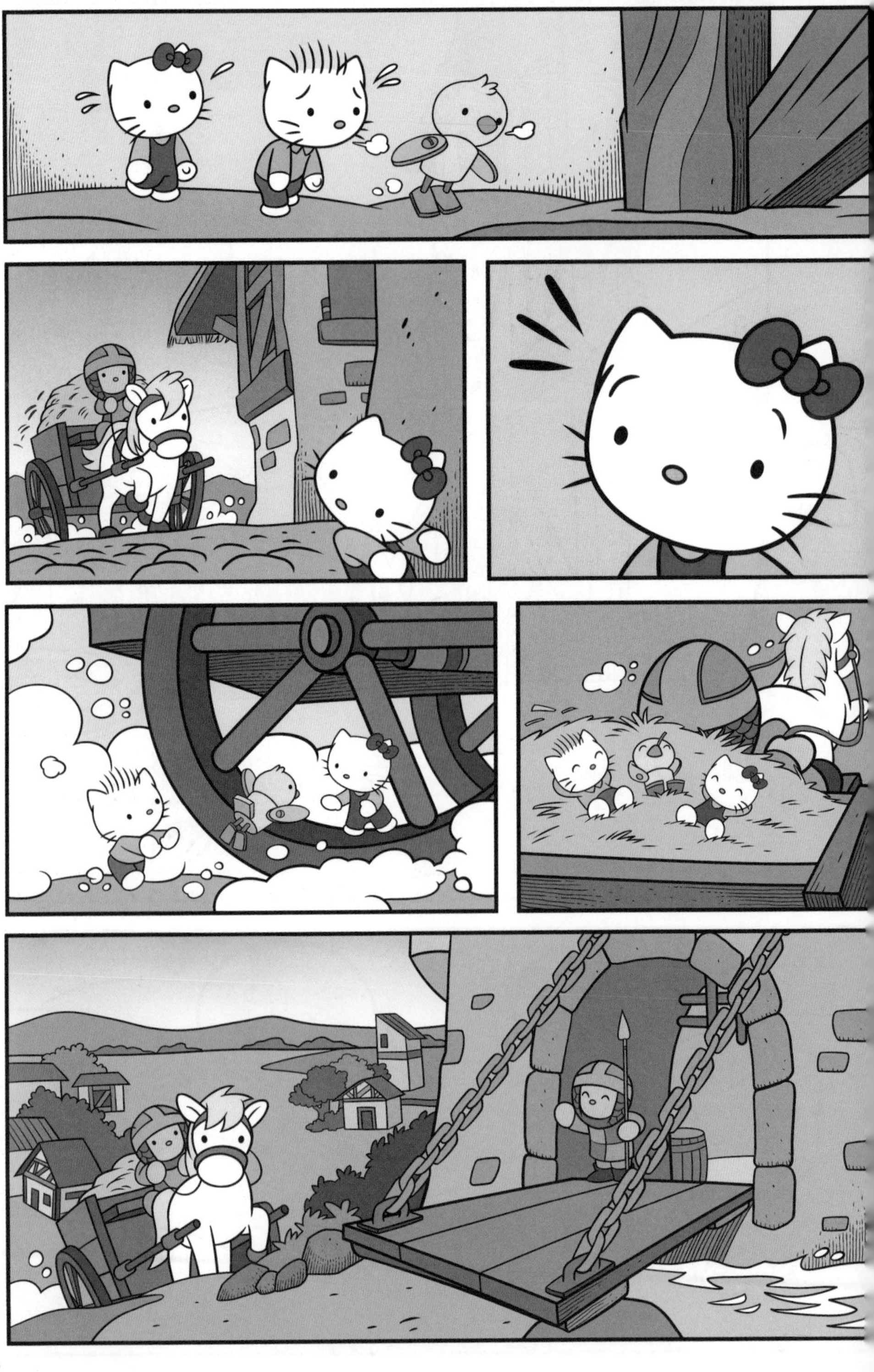

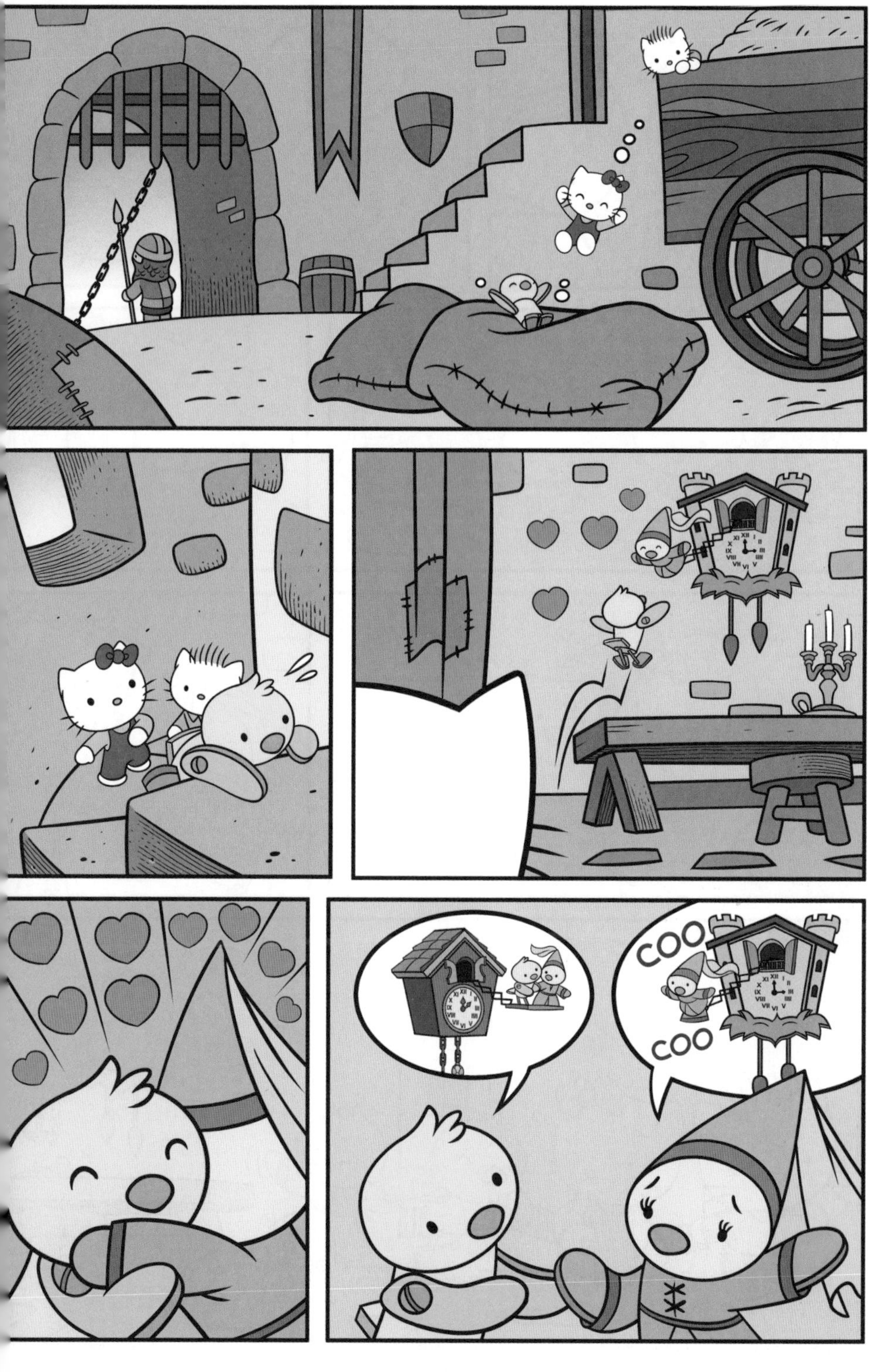
COO
COO

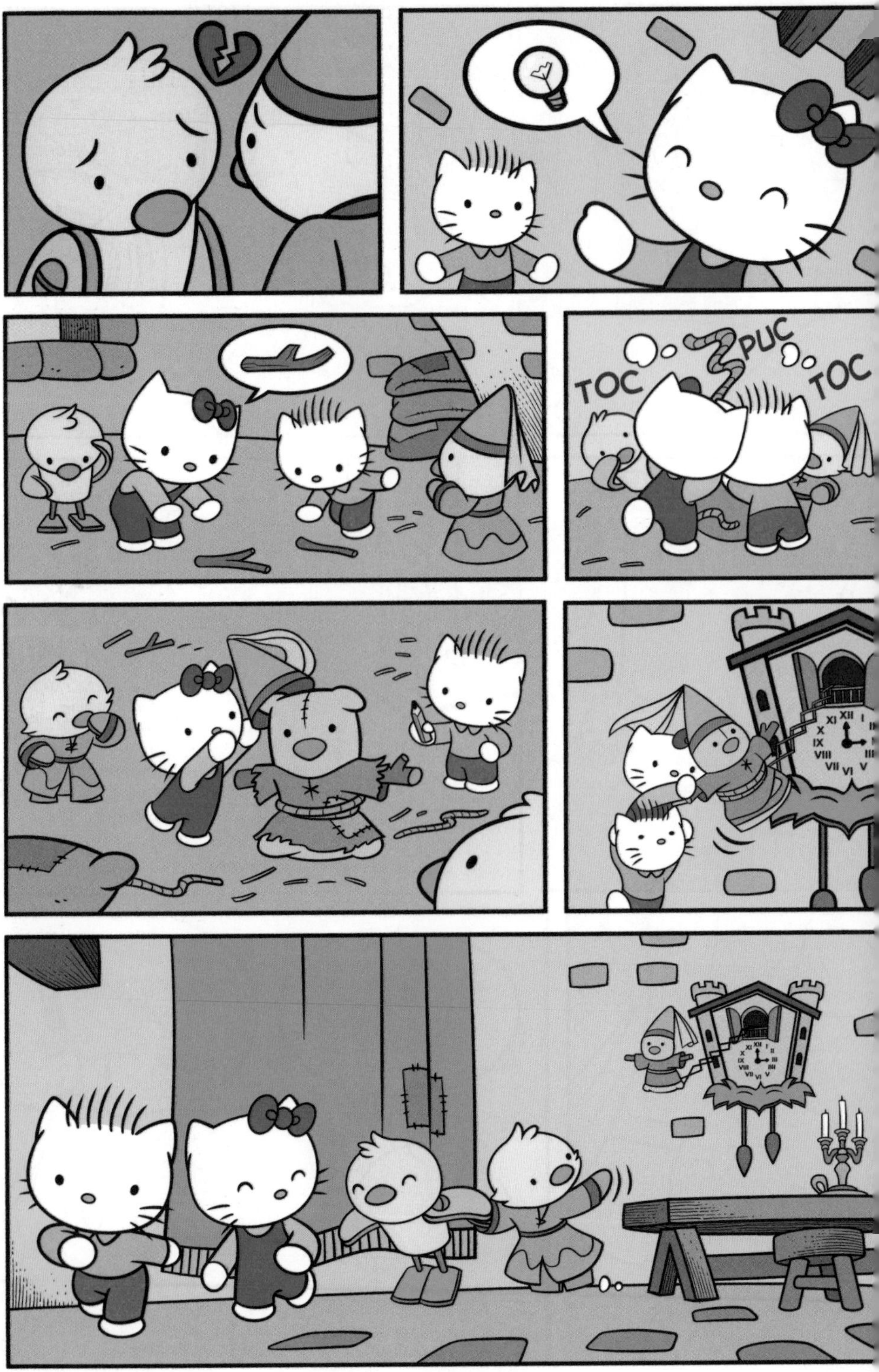
TOC
PUC
TOC

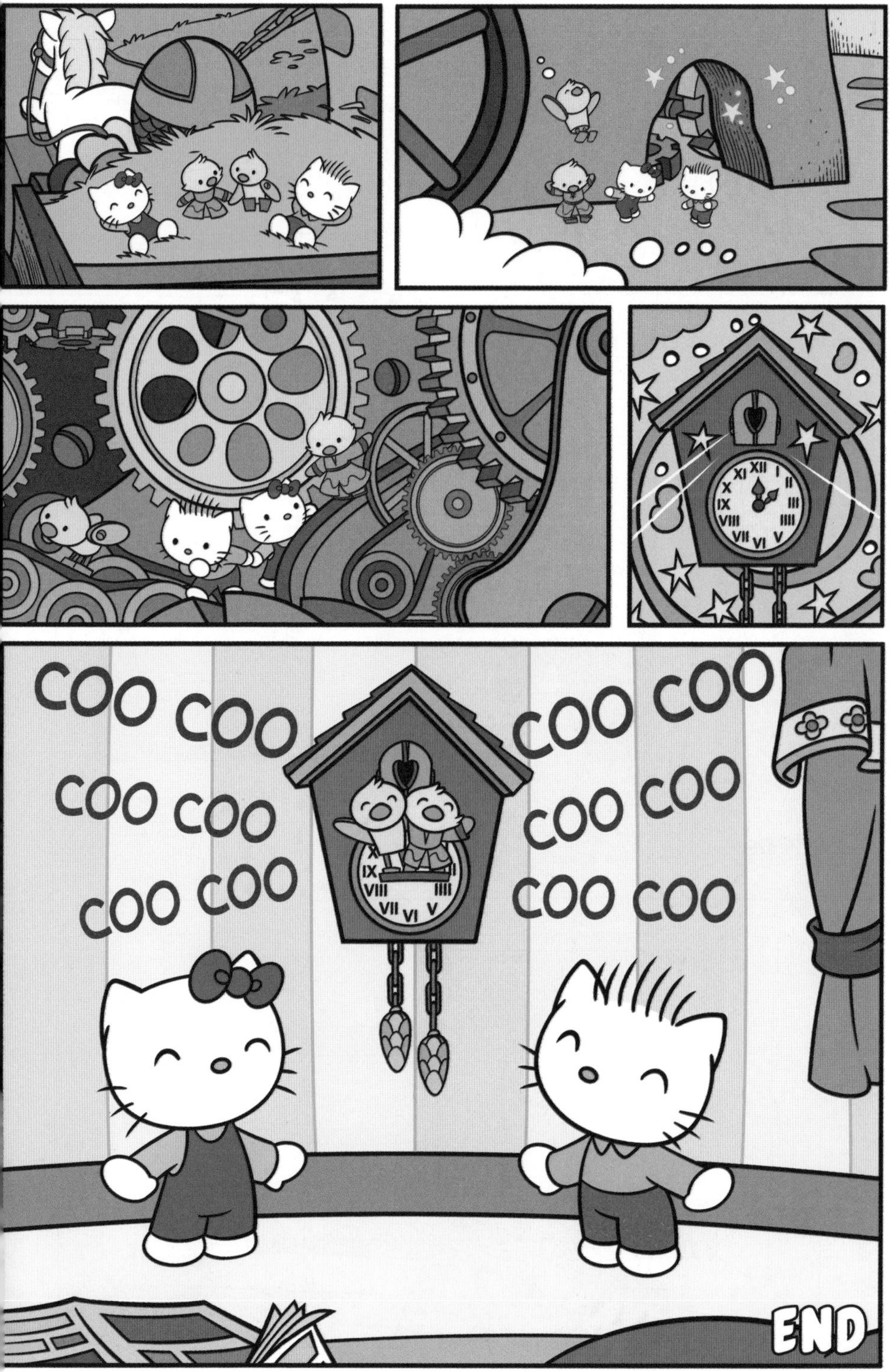
COO COO
COO COO
COO COO
COO COO
COO COO
COO COO
END

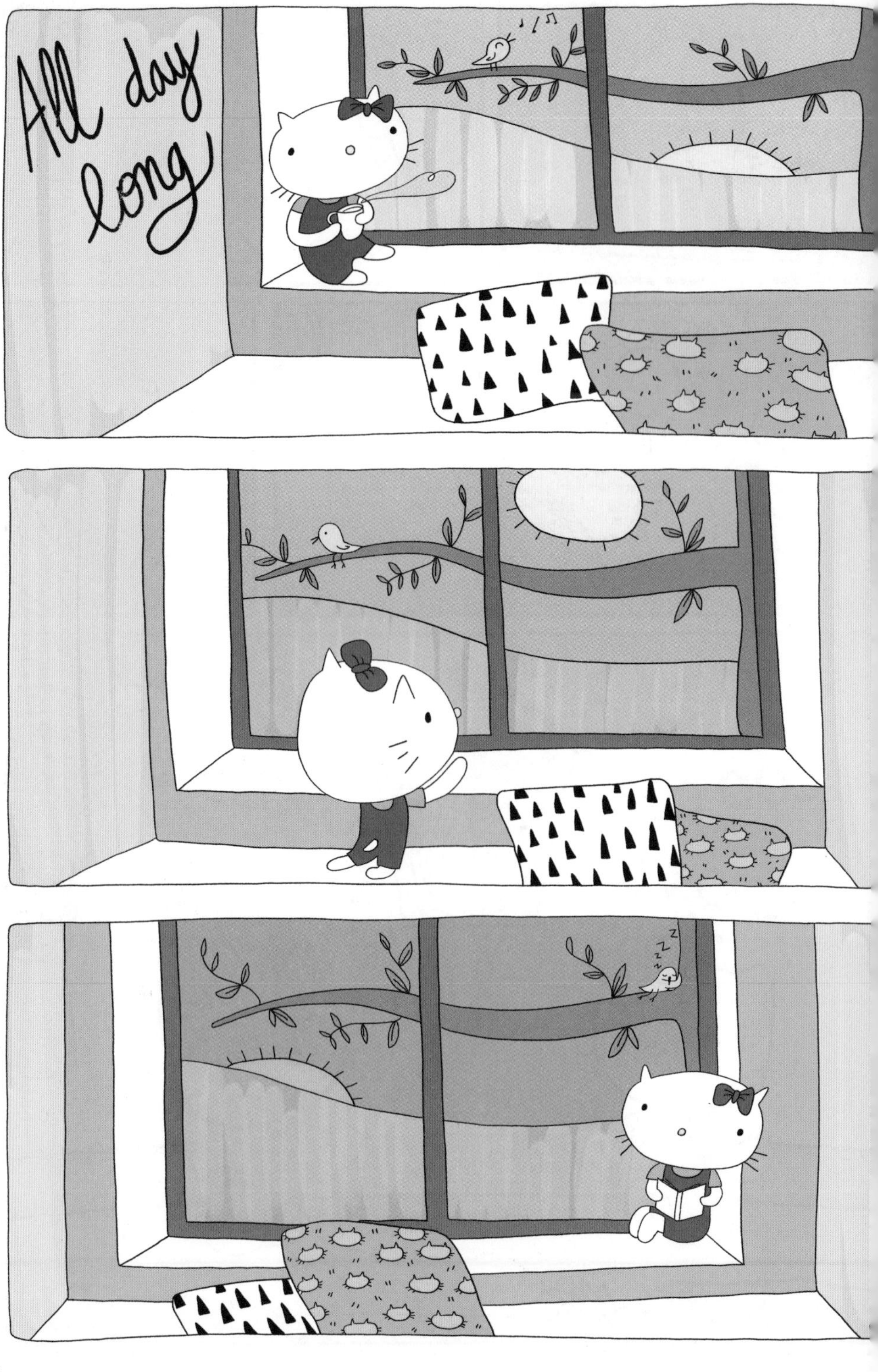
All day long

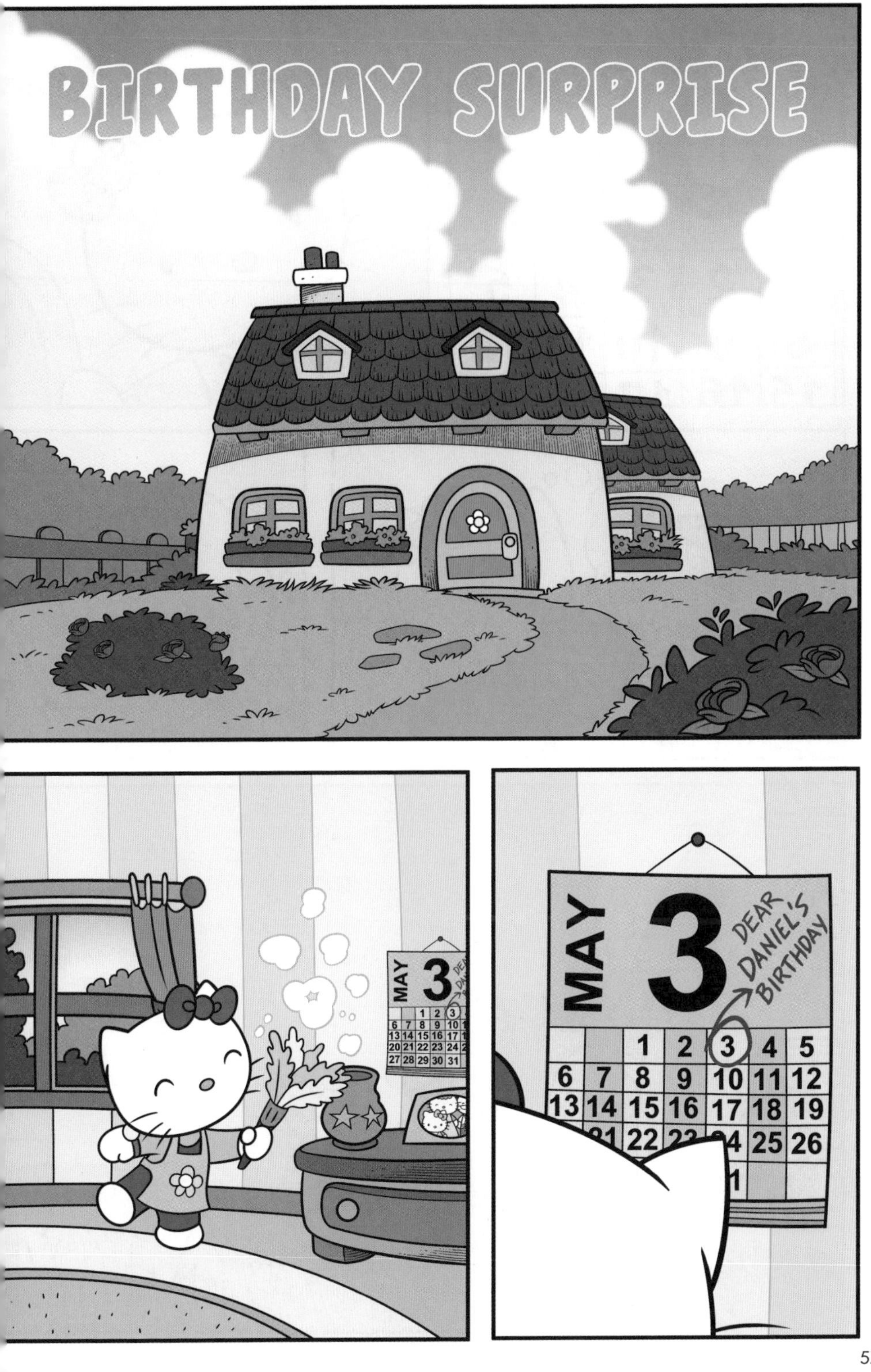
BIRTHDAY SURPRISE
MAY 3
DEAR DANIEL'S BIRTHDAY

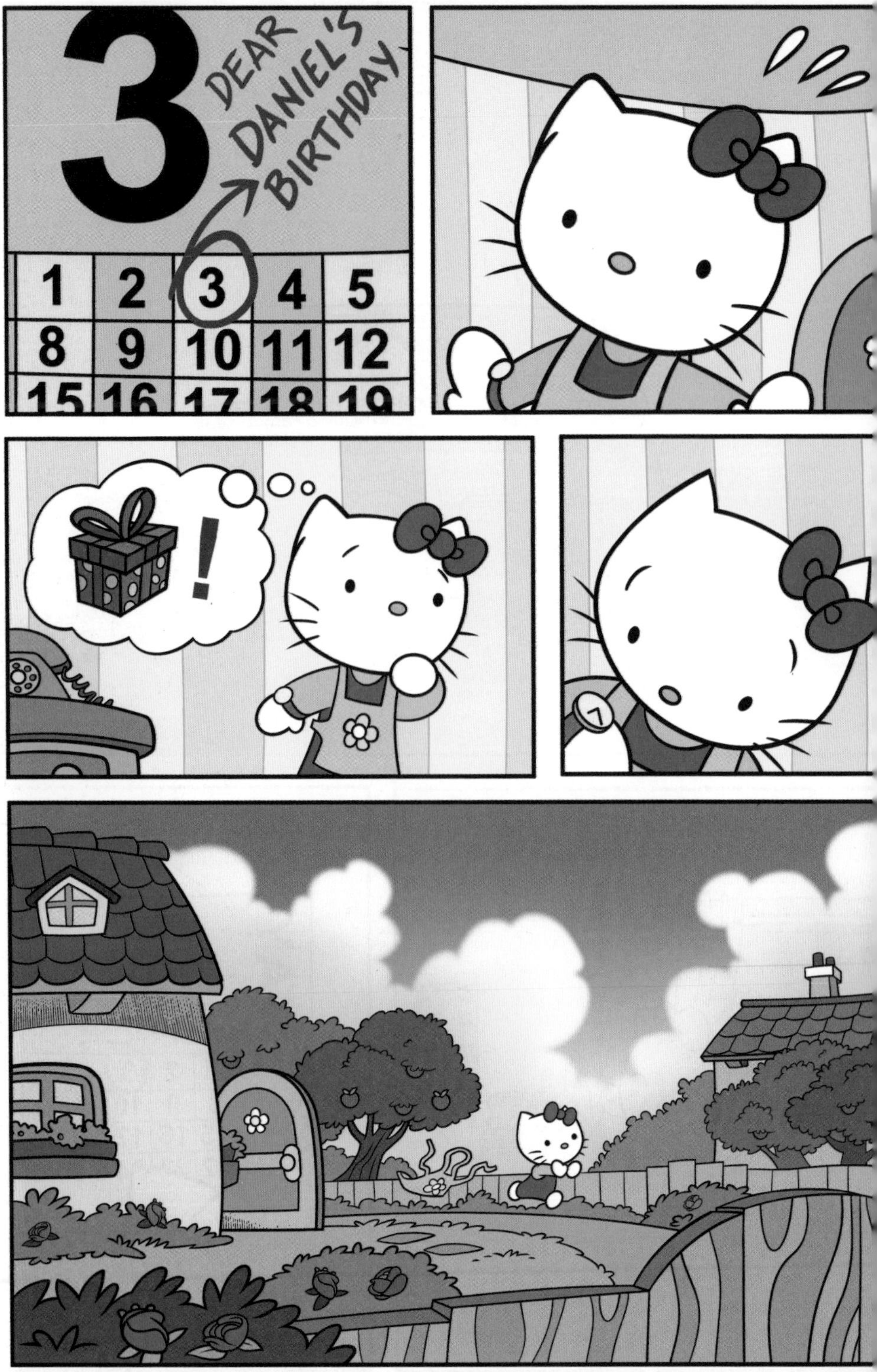
3
DEAR DANIEL'S BIRTHDAY
1 2 3 4 5
8 9 10 11 12
15 16 17 18 19
!

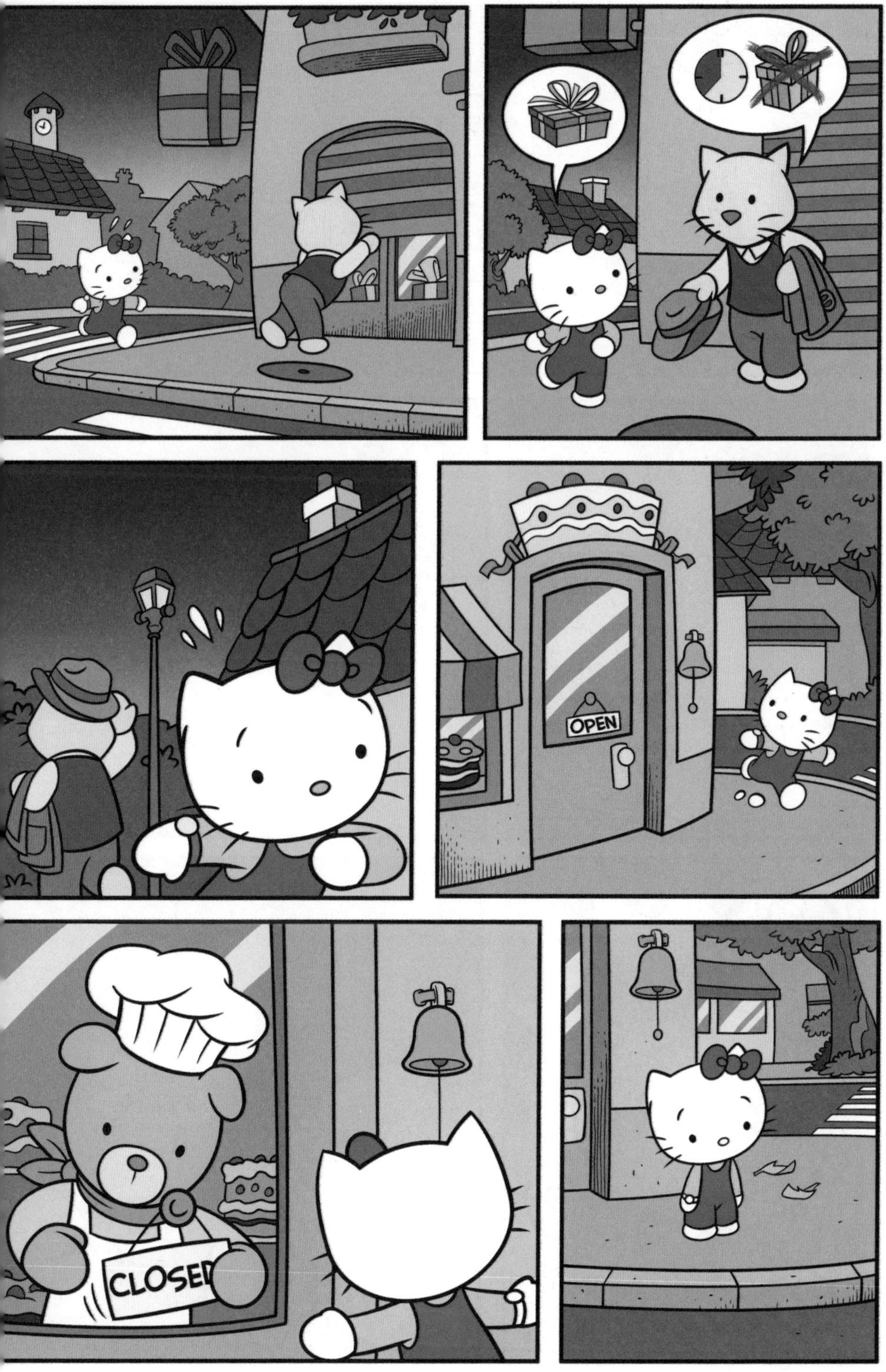
OPEN
CLOSED

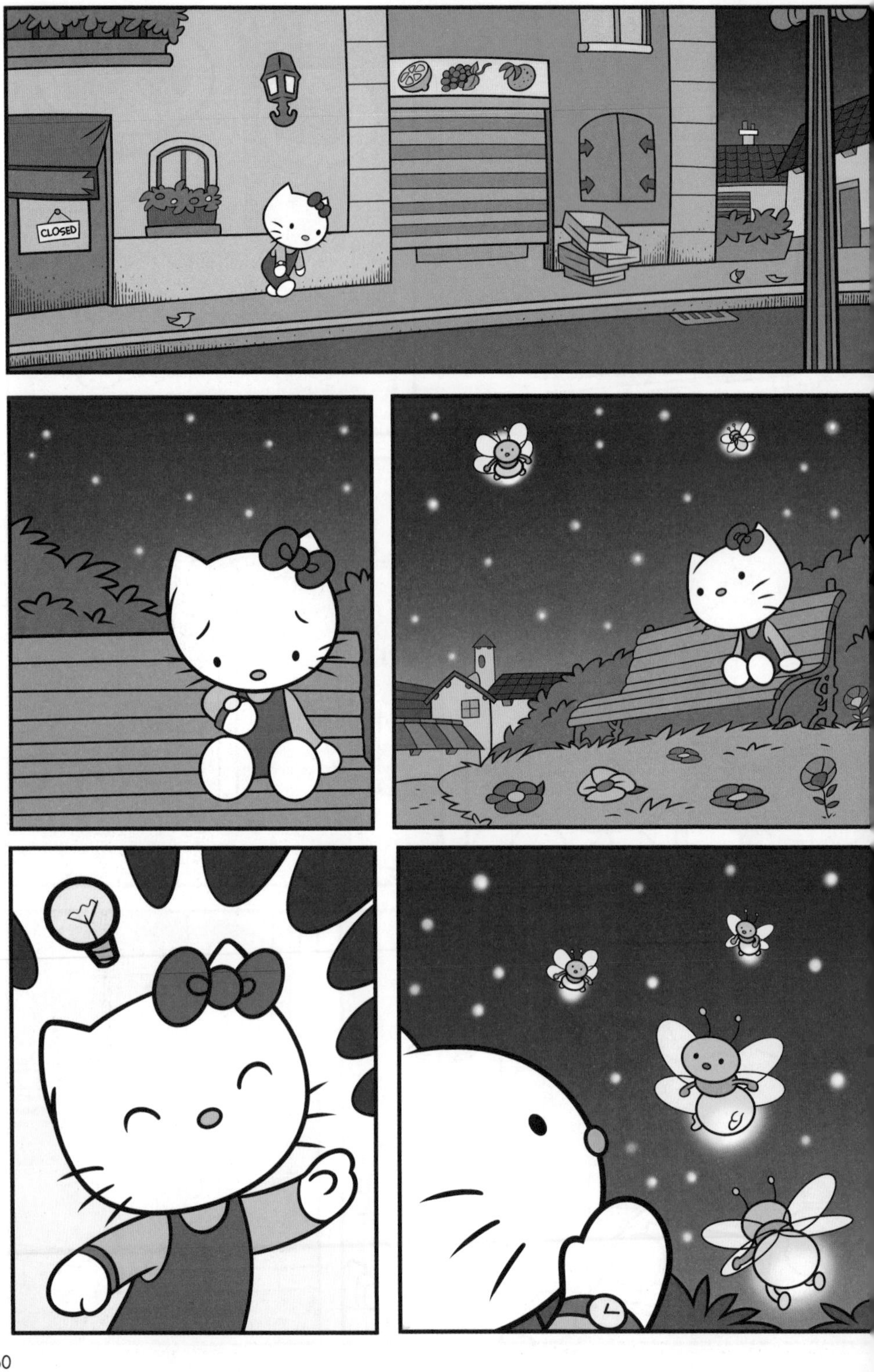
CLOSED

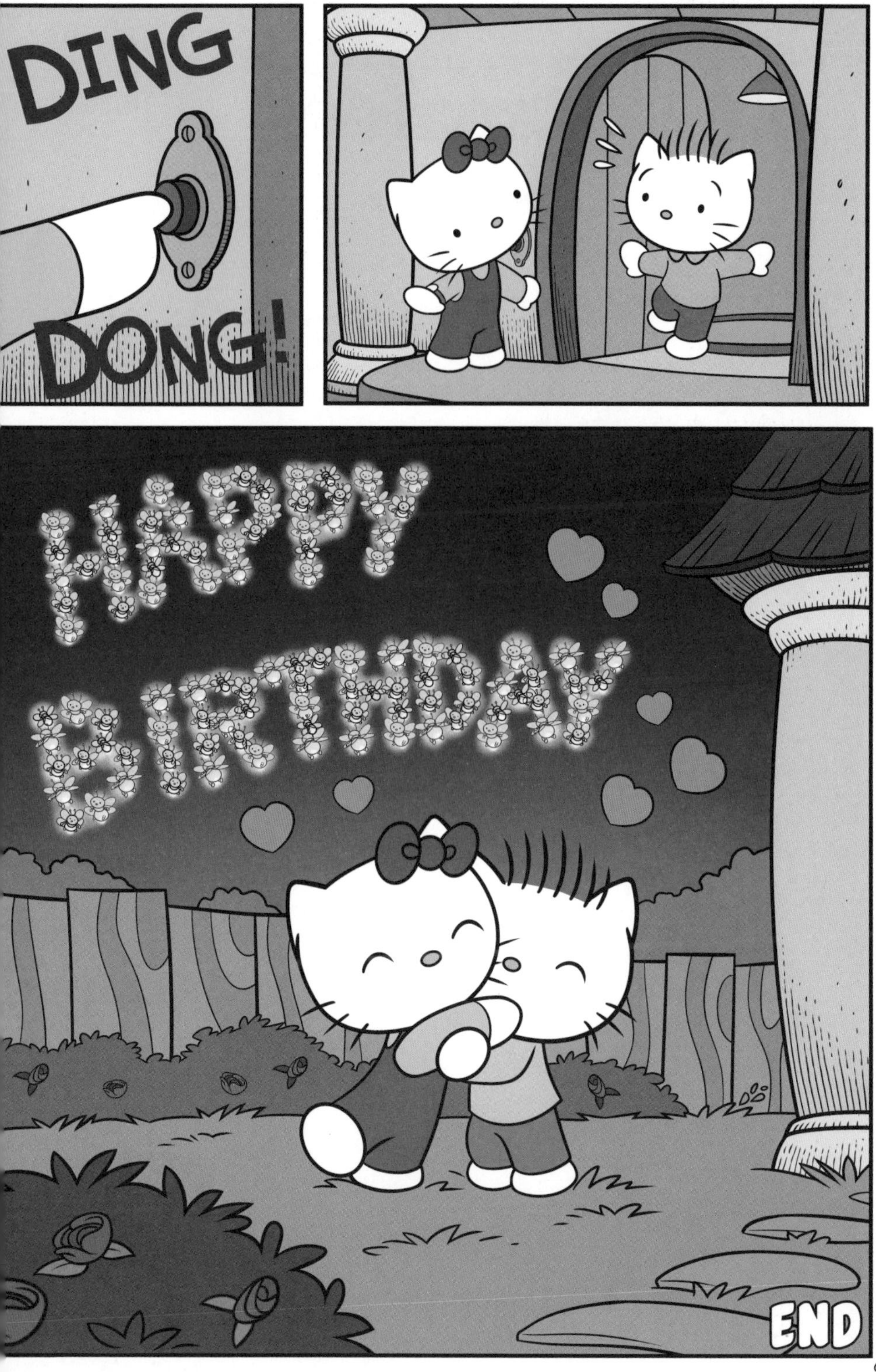
DING
DONG!
HAPPY BIRTHDAY
END

Creators

Giovanni Castro was born in Colombia, studied art there, and now lives and works in Barcelona, Spain. He works mainly in editorial illustration and comics, which he loves a lot. He used to work with traditional media, but nowadays he does his illustrations digitally. He loves science fiction and historical themes and is interested in history, art and languages.

Jacob Chabot is a New York City-based cartoonist and illustrator. His comics have appeared in publications such as *Nickelodeon Magazine*, *Mad Magazine*, *Spongebob Comics*, and various Marvel titles. He also illustrated *Voltron Force: Shelter from the Storm* and *Voltron Force: True Colors* for VIZ Media. His comic *The Mighty Skullboy Army* is published through Dark Horse and in 2008 was nominated for an Eisner Award for Best Book for Teens.

Jorge Monlongo makes comic books, editorial and children's illustrations and video game designs and paints on canvas and walls. He combines traditional and digital techniques to create worlds in beautiful colors that usually hide terrible secrets. You can see his works in the press (*El Pais*, *Muy interesante*, *Rolling Stone*) and read his comic book series, *Mameshiba*, published by VIZ Media in the USA.

Ian McGinty lives in Savannah, Georgia, and also parts of the universe! Also, Earth. When he isn't drawing comics and rad pictures of octopuses (octopi?), he's laughing at funny-looking dogs and making low-carb burritos! Ian draws stuff for VIZ Media, Top Shelf Productions, BOOM! Studios, Zenescope and many more cool folk! But he cannot draw garbage trucks for some reason.

Erica Salcedo is a freelance illustrator living in the peaceful town of Cuenca (Spain). Her work is focused on children's illustration inspired by her everyday life. Her imagination does the rest. Her style is a mixture of hand drawing with digital techniques, simply executed with a pinch of humor. She loves drawing (obviously), traveling, animals, drinking tea every day, eating sweets, and not taking life too seriously.

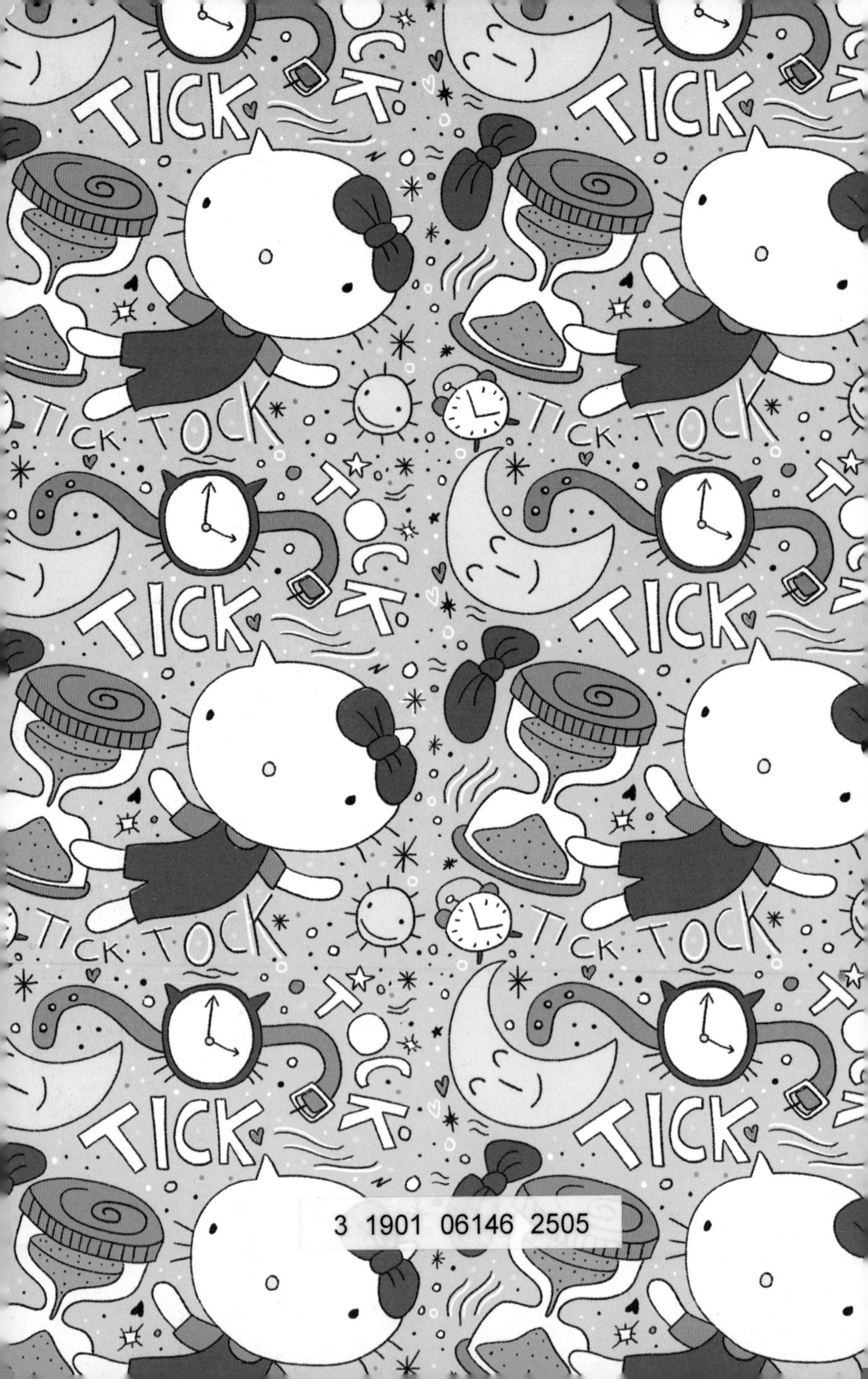
TICK TOCK